We Gon' Ride 2
Cobain & Keri

The FINALE

BY: ZAII

Where we last left off…

I carried her slowly down the steps as she silently cried in my chest. Hearing her cry was doing something to my manhood. I was pissed that she even had to go through this shit. Once we got to the front of the house, I instantly stopped when I came face to face with a gun, but what was confusing me was the person holding the gun.

"Shyne, what the hell are you doing here?" I barked.

"Is this the friend that you told my daughter that you wanted her to meet one day?" She asked with tears falling from her eyes.

"This isn't the time or the place for us to be having this conversation Shyne," I yelled.

"That's the problem it's never the right time or place for us to EVER have this conversation, Cobain," She yelled pointing the gun between the both of us.

"Can you stand?" I asked Keri.

She nodded her head up and down, so I slowly placed her down on her feet and leaned her up against the wall.

"YOU SEE HOW YOU ARE SO LOVING AND GENTLE WITH HER, WHY CAN'T YOU BE LIKE THAT WITH ME? I HAVE ALWAYS LOVED YOU," She screamed.

I slowly walked towards her with my hands up because I didn't want to make the mistake of scaring her then the gun goes off.

"Shyne listen to me; we go through this all the time. You are the mother of my daughter nothing more, nothing less. We are co-parenting Kaylee that's it," I stated.

"NO… NO… that's not it. I do everything you ask of me; I cook, clean, I suck your dick and fuck you whenever you want. I haven't had a man since I had Kaylee," She explained.

"Shyne you chose to do those things, they were never forced, but at the same time, I made sure you never wanted for anything. As for dating you could have been had a man, YOU chose not to get one," I reasoned with her still getting closer.

"I don't want any of that, all I wanted was you, I love you for you not for what you can do for me," She cried.

I looked back at Keri, mad that she even had to hear all this shit and that I had placed her in a fucked-up situation. I looked back at Shyne, and when she wiped the falling tears, I used that as my opportunity to try and take the gun from her. I grabbed her wrist and tried to take the gun from her we wrestled for a minute because she had a grip on the gun.

"Let me gooooooo Cobain," She shouted.

"POP" Was all that was heard when the gun went off.

"NOOOOOOOOOOOO," I heard Keri yell.

Chapter 1- Keri

"OH MY GOD COBAIN," I yelled out trying to make my way down the steps to see if they were okay, it was so much blood I was starting to get nervous.

I was in so much pain, but I pushed through to make it over to them. I wasn't sure what to expect as I got closer.

"Cobain?" I called as I got closer to them.

I held my breath the closer I got to them, I kneeled and checked for a pulse.

"I'm good doc," I heard him say in a low tone.

"Oh, thank God," I spoke releasing the breath I was holding.

I tried to help him up as best as I could considering how I was feeling. Once he was up, we both looked down at Shyne, and she was bleeding.

"FUCKKKKKKK SHYNE," He yelled out in frustration.

"Ahhhhh, help me," She cried out in labored breaths.

I watched as he picked her up and carried her to the car then placed her in the backseat closing the door. He then jogged over to me and looked me in the eyes.

"Listen doc I need to take her to the hospital, I know you're in pain too, but I really need to get her to the hospital. If you don't want to go I can drop you to my place and wait for me to come back," He suggested.

I thought about what he was saying for a second before I responded. The pain I was feeling was minor compared to what was going on right now.

"I'll ride with you to take her to the hospital," I told him.

"You sure?" He asked with uneasy eyes.

"Yes, now let's go before she bleeds out in the back of your car," I replied walking towards his car.

We both got in the car, and I looked back at his daughter's mother and couldn't believe the lengths she'd go to make this man love her. As bad as I wanted to say fuck her for pointing that gun at me, the doctor in me wouldn't allow her to die on my watch.

"Do you have any clothes in here I can use? I need to try and control this bleeding before she bleeds to death," I stated.

He hopped out his car and jogged to the trunk and came back with a gym bag full of clothes. He opened it up and handed me a few pieces, I climbed over the seat and sat in the back then placed the shirt over her stomach to control the bleeding.

"We need to get her to the hospital, the bullet is still lodged in her stomach, and it needs to be removed before it travels anywhere and kills her," I told him truthfully.

He put the car in drive and sped off straight to the hospital, I tried to apply pressure as best as I could without disturbing the bullet and making it travel any further. I just stared at her wondering if I would ever love a man that much that I would risk my life and the lives of others just to get him to love me the way I deserved.

"Aye doc?" Cobain called out bringing me from my thoughts.

"Yes,"

"I know it's a lot to ask of you, but I need a favor from you," He stated.

"What's up?' I responded.

"When we get to the hospital if anyone asks I will tell them this is my daughter's mom and I stopped by to get something from her before our date, and we found her like this," He explained as he kept glancing at me through the rearview mirror.

"Okay," I agreed.

"Thanks, doc," He replied.

We continued to drive to the hospital in silence while I tried to control the bleeding.

"Please don't let me die," She pleaded as the tears slowly falling from her eyes.

"I'll do my best to make sure that you don't," I told her with a smile.

We pulled up to the hospital, and he put the car in park and jumped out then ran straight inside. A few seconds later he came running back out with a couple of nurses behind him with a gurney. They slid her from the back and rushed her right inside the emergency room; this shit was starting to feel like déjà vu to me. Cobain walked over and helped me out the car then wrapped his arms around me as we entered the hospital.

We walked and sat in the waiting room as we waited for a doctor to let us know what was going on.

"Thanks, doc," Cobain spoke breaking the silence between us.

"No problem," I replied smiling at him.

"How are you feeling?" He questioned looking at me.

"I'm okay, and thank you for coming I know you didn't have to," I acknowledged.

"You know I got you, I told you that already," He stated.

I looked at him and smiled, he was just so handsome and not like anything I expected him to be. We continued to sit in silence and wait for some news on his daughter's mother.

"You know when I catch your fiancé that nigga is dead right?" He spoke randomly.

I didn't even bother to respond to him, whatever happens to Max now he brought on to himself, and there wasn't anything I could do to about it.

Chapter 2- Cree

I woke up from being tasered, and everything around me was black, I tried not to panic, but I felt like I couldn't breathe with this sack over my head. I slowed down my breathing and got my thoughts together as I tried to figure out a way out of this. All I could tell was that I was tied to a chair with my arms and feet bound to each side. I heard some footsteps and stopped breathing.

"Look who's awake," I heard a voice say making me jump a little.

Next thing I know the sheet that was over my head was taken off and I found myself adjusting to the light. When I was finally able to focus, I was face to face with the man that had scheduled the fake appointment, and I just stared at him with so much hate in my eyes.

"What do you want from me?" I questioned with venom spewing from my mouth.

"From you nothing, but your little boyfriend I want to make him and his friend pay for taking the life of someone close to me. Just call it an eye for an eye," He spoke with an evil smile.

"What does that have to do with me?"

"You see you are the closest thing to him besides Cobain, Ali never keeps a female around for long so when we saw that he was still dealing with you a light bulb went off and here you are," He said like it was nothing.

"HELPPPPPPPP MEEEEEEE, ANYBODY I'M DOWN HERE, CAN YOU HEAR ME?" I yelled out hoping someone heard me.

"Don't waste your breath pretty lady, where we are can't anyone hear you," He laughed.

"I just want to go home," I cried.

"You will, the way I look at it when Ali comes, he won't be alone, and so I will have a two for one special. Once I kill them both you can go free my dear," He said with a smirk, but I knew he was lying.

I closed my eyes and said a silent prayer that I made it out of this situation alive, and if I did, I was leaving Ali alone for good. This is the exact reason why I didn't want to deal with thugs it was always something, and now I'm here caught in between something that has absolutely nothing to do with me.

"To show you I'm not a complete asshole; I'll even feed you as long as you promise not to try no shit, because I would really hate to kill you before your knight in shining sweatpants comes and saves you," He threatened.

I nodded my head agreeing with what he was saying but at the first opportunity that presented itself I was going to try to escape, there's no way I was trusting this man not to kill me at his leisure.

He walked out, and another man walked in sitting in the chair that was across the room and all he did was stare at me and it creeped me the fuck out.

"Do you know how beautiful you are?" He asked looking at me with a disgusting look on his face as he licked his chapped ass lips.

I didn't even bother to respond to him, I just rolled my eyes and looked around as I tried to figure out a way from this hell hole. I was pretty much stuck and didn't know what I was going to do but sitting here just waiting wasn't an option.

"How did your chocolate ass even get caught up in this shit?"

"Please don't speak to me," I responded looking at him. If looks could kill his ass would be dead right now.

"You might want to be nice to me, I may or may not help you get out of this situation," He spoke with a smirk on his face.

I looked at him with pure disgust, even if I was that desperate I still wouldn't allow him to help me out this place. I closed my eyes and said a silent prayer that I would be out of this situation sooner than later. I didn't even know what time of day it was or anything, I'm sure Keri was worried sick right now about where I was.

Chapter 3- Cobain

As I was sitting in this waiting room waiting to see what was up with Shyne's ass, I couldn't help but think about the condition that I found Keri in. Shit wasn't sitting well with me at all. After I made sure Shyne's stupid ass was good, I was going to go see what was up with this nigga Max, as a matter of fact let me shoot my man a text so he could run me his background.

"How you feeling?"

"I'm okay, feeling much better," She replied looking over at me with a weak smile.

"You sure?" I questioned looking at her seriously.

"Yes, I promise," She said smiling at me.

We sat there in silence waiting to hear from the doctor, with so much going on I forgot that I was looking for clues as to where Cree was being held at. I was debating on if I should even tell Keri what was going on right now considering everything that just happened.

"Excuse me I need to make a call," I told her walking out the waiting room.

"Okay,"

I kissed her on the forehead and left out the room to check in with Ali, I dialed his number and waited for him to pick up.

"Yo tell me you got something bro," Was the first thing he said as soon as the phone connected.

"Nah not yet, some shit came up," I admitted.

"Some shit came up, what the fuck you mean? What happened?" He yelled.

"Calm down bro, I'll tell you,"

I started telling him what happened after I hung up with him earlier and how I ended up in the ER now.

"ARE YOU FUCKIN KIDDIN' ME RIGHT NOW?" He yelled so loud making me pull the phone away from my ear.

"Yeah man, shit got real over here," I replied shaking my head still in disbelief my damn self.

"Yo Shyne needs her ass beat for that corny shit she pulled now she back there fighting for her life and where the fuck is baby girl at?" He asked sounding pissed the fuck off; He didn't play when it came to Kaylee at all.

"That's a good damn question, soon as her ass wakes up, I will ask her. I can't believe she really pulled this shit."

"How's Keri holding up?" He asked trying to change the subject.

"She's hanging in there, for the most part, but you know that nigga is a dead man walking," I spoke in a low tone.

"I already know, you ain't even saying nothing. Did you let shorty know what's going on?"

" I didn't. I don't even know how to bring this shit up to her. I think this will be a little too much for her at one time. First she gets into it with her nigga, and then on the rescue, my crazy ass baby mother comes and tries to take us out, but ends up shooting her damn self. Then to have to tell that her best friend was kidnapped and we don't even have a clue as to where she might be at. Any real person would have a mental breakdown after all that shit," I stated rubbing my hand across my face.

"Yeah, I feel you, but she needs to know, especially with what she just went through. I can almost guarantee you that she's going to call her to vent," He stated, making me think about what he was saying.

"Shit, you're right. Aight, let me go handle this, and I'll hit you back. Keep me posted on your moves because I know your ass isn't sitting still much longer," I laughed knowing he was home going crazy right now. He was like a toddler with ADHD and didn't do well with idle time.

"Nigga you don't know me," He chuckled.

"You think I don't, but go do what you do and just keep me posted," I replied hanging up.

I put my head down and took a deep breath preparing myself for the conversation that I was about to have with Keri. I was still getting to know her and wasn't really sure how she was going to react to the news. I walked back into the waiting room and just looked at Keri; she was just so damn beautiful, like a classic beauty that you saw in them old school movies. I walked over to her and sat down.

"Hey is everything okay?" She asked as soon as I sat down.

"Yeah, that was Ali, listen there's something that I need to talk to you about" I spoke grabbing her hand and squeezing it before pulling it up to my mouth to kiss it.

"Okay, what's up?" She asked looking over at me with a nervous look on her face.

"Okay before I tell you just know that everything is under control," I started.

"What is going on Cobain? You're making me nervous," She responded with a shaky voice.

"I'm not one to beat around the bush, but at the same time, I haven't really cared about nobody's feelings in a long while except for Kaylee's. So, with that being said, I'm going to just come right out and say it... Cree is missing," I blurted out.

"WHAT?" She yelled out in shock.

"Shhhhh, calm down," I tried to say.

"CALM DOWN? ARE YOU FUCKIN' SERIOUS RIGHT NOW? HOW DO YOU EXPECT ME TO CALM DOWN WHEN YOU JUST TOLD ME MY FRIEND WAS MISSING?" She screamed on the verge of tears.

"Ma I know this is a lot for you to deal with right now, but what I need from you is to stay calm and keep your voice down," I spoke in a harsh whisper.

She looked around the waiting area to see if anyone heard her yell out, then she focused back on me waiting for me to explain which I did. By the time I was done the tears were coming down her beautiful face.

"Keri, I promise you that we are working hard to locate her and bring her home," I assured her.

She didn't immediately respond she just sat there while the silent tears fell from her face, making me feel like shit even more than I already did.

"Keri, just trust me. I got you," I stated.

She nodded her head up and down as I pulled her into me and she laid her head on my shoulder and I kissed her forehead.

"You promise to bring her home safe?" She asked in a whisper.

I really didn't want to promise her that because I really wasn't sure what we were going up against but anything to possibly bring a smile back to her face I was down to do.

"I promise Keri,"

"Okay," She responded.

I continued to rub her shoulder as we sat here waiting to hear back from the doctors on Shyne's condition.

Chapter 4- Ali

Shit was all the way fucked up right now, it was like the enemy was attacking us from all angles and we were just taking hits across the board. Since I knew Cobain was wrapped up right now, it was up to me to get out and shake some shit up. I grabbed my keys and was ready to go put this work in. I opened my door, and there was one of my little niggas standing there about to knock.

"What the hell your little ass doing here?" I questioned looking at him crazy.

"Cobain told me to drop this off to you," He responded handing me a new iPhone 7 out of the bag he was carrying.

"Oh shit, good looks my nigga," I replied giving him dap.

He nodded his head and turned and walked away, I closed the door behind me and walked to my car, I got inside and started to program my phone as soon as it was up and running it began to ring.

"Yo,"

I didn't hear anything, I pulled the phone from my ear and looked at it making sure the person was still there.

"Who is this?" I yelled still waiting for a reply, and that's when I heard it.

"AHHHHHHHHH, PLEASE STOP, GET OFF ME, HELPPPP ME PLEASE ANYONE," I heard Cree yelling making my blood boil.

"Ali my friend how's it going?" Dragon spoke casually into the phone.

"You stupid mother fucker," I seethed.

"Calm down my friend, I just want to talk," He responded coolly.

"Talk? Nigga, you about to be talking to my gun when I find your ass, you better not had touched a hair on her head either," I threatened.

"I don't think you're in the right position to be making idle threats," He chuckled then that's when I heard Cree scream again.

"DON'T TOUCH ME,"

"A hair on her head should be the least of your problems, we are over here having a good time getting to know each other," He laughed into the phone.

Before I could respond, I heard her voice come through the phone.

"Ali?" She said weakly through tears.

"Cree baby I'm coming for you," I responded.

"Please come get me now."

"I'm working on it baby I promise, just stay strong. I'll be there soon," I promised.

"Ali, please hurry," Was the last thing I heard before the phone hung up on me.

"FUCKKKKKKKKKK," I yelled banging on the steering wheel.

This shit was becoming too much for me, I was about to turn into a beast, and once he's out, he wasn't going away until Cree was back home and everyone that had something to do with her disappearance was dealt with. I put my car in drive and pulled off straight to her office; I don't care what the fuck Cobain said I was getting inside.

I pulled out my phone and hit up one of my tech guys.

"Yo I need a solid," I spoke into the phone as soon as he picked up.

"You got it, name it," He replied.

"I need you to find me any family member of this nigga Dragon. I don't care where they're at or who it is, find them and then shoot me their locations. This nigga thinks I'm playing I got a trick for his ass," I stated.

"Copy, bro already on it. Give me about thirty minutes, and I'll have something," He replied.

"Say less," I replied hanging up the phone.

I pressed down on the gas and went straight to Cree's job. I swear it felt like I got there in ten minutes. I jumped out my car and walked up to the door, and it was still locked, I peeked through the glass and saw that nobody was inside. I walked back to my car and grabbed my gun from the secret compartment in my car, I pulled it out and attached the silencer to it before I walked around the back.

I looked around before raising the gun and shooting the locks off, I pushed the door open and walked inside. I hit the light switch cutting them on and started looking around to see if I could find anything that could lead me to Cree's location. I went behind the front desk and opened all the drawers looking for anything, I pulled out a calendar book and saw a bunch of names, times, and locations and then that's when I spotted Cree's name and appointment time and location. I ripped the paper out the book stuffed in my pocket and left right out the way I came in.

I jumped in my car and put the address in my GPS and saw it was about thirty minutes from here but the way my adrenaline was running I would get there in fifteen. I put the car in drive and sped off to the destination.

I pulled up to a house and looked around to check the neighborhood out and make sure this was the right house; this house didn't look like someone was being held captive inside of it. I shut the car off and grabbed my gun and got out the car and made my way up the steps to the door. I looked around then I picked my foot up and kicked the door open then pointed my gun inside before walking in, I let my gun lead the way.

I walked all around the house and saw no signs that anyone was here, I was starting to get frustrated. I came back downstairs and walked towards the kitchen and saw a door that led to a basement. I opened the door and made my way slowly down the steps. When I got to the bottom, I immediately got pissed.

"FUCKKKKKKKK MAN."

Chapter 5- Keri

As I sat here trying to be strong, I was dying on the inside. Between Cree being missing, Khloe in the hospital and Max in the wind after beating me, I was tired and didn't know how much more of this I could take. I was trying to hold it together but was slowly falling apart. I laid there with my head on Cobain's shoulder and said a prayer up for my best friend that she made it out of whatever is going on alive because I don't know what I would do without her.

"You okay Keri?" Cobain asked bringing me from my thoughts.

"Yeah, I'm okay" I lied.

"I know we haven't known each other long, but I read people very well. That's something you will learn the more time we spend together, so I know when someone is lying to me," He stated.

I took a deep breath and thought about what I wanted to say to him.

"I'm not okay, I'm tired and scared," I admitted.

I felt his breathing stop a little before he started again, he was trying hard to control his breathing and maybe his anger.

"Keri listen to me and listen to me well, I don't ever want to hear you EVER say that you're scared when you're around me. You should never feel that emotion while you're in my presence. I told you I would NEVER let anything happen to you, you have my word," He stated in a serious tone.

I nodded my head up and down saying that I heard him, but as much as I wanted to believe him it was hard especially coming from my situation. I was feeling him, but I had to make sure I was feeling him because I saw myself with him and not because he saved me from my situation.

"Now if you're tired I can get you a ride to my place and you can wait for me there until I leave from up here," He spoke as he rubbed my thigh.

"No, it's fine I'll wait with you," I smiled.

"You sure? It's no problem at all," He assured me.

"I promise," I replied looking up at him.

"Family of Shyne Myers," A doctor walked over to us with papers in his hand.

We both stood up and waited to see what he was going to say next.

"I'm Doctor Lovejoy, I was the surgeon that operated on Ms. Myers," He introduced.

"I'm Cobain, and this is Keri," He replied shaking his hand.

"Dr. Anderson," He nodded his head at me.

"Hello," I spoke with a smile.

"So, what's the deal doc?" Cobain questioned getting right to the point.

"I'm going to give y'all some privacy," I said about to walk away.

"Don't go, I want you here with me," He replied grabbing my hand.

"No, it's fine, you're in good hands with this one right here. I'm going to go check on my sister," I told him.

He looked at me like he didn't really want me to go but I needed to go check on my sister and besides his daughter's mom wasn't none of my business.

"Okay," He reluctantly agreed.

"I'll be back," I winked walking off leaving him and the doctor alone.

I walked to the elevator and pressed it then waited for it to come, once the doors opened I got in and pressed down instead of up. I was in dire need of some coffee before I did anything else tonight. I walked into the cafeteria and made myself a cup of coffee then sat down at a corner table just to get my thoughts together. I needed a moment to myself just to think and see what's going on with my life. I feel like my life has been on 100 since I opened my eyes, and I just needed a TIME OUT. I took a few sips and put my head down for a minute and enjoyed this alone time even if it was only for a second.

After a few minute's I picked my head up grabbed my coffee and made my way to my sister's room. When I got to her room an overwhelming feeling came over me, she was laying in the bed sleeping so peacefully hooked up to all these monitors. I felt so guilty the closer I got to her bed, it was my fault she was even in this hospital bed right now.

I pulled up a chair and sat next to the bed and just looked at her, I picked up her hand and squeezed it. The longer I looked at her, the more emotional I got. My sister was back in the same place that I told her I never wanted to see her to be at again, but this time she was here because of a man that I once chose to love. I couldn't help the tears that fell from my eyes. This was my baby sister and I was supposed to protect her and when I thought I was doing the right thing it backfired and blew up in my face.

I felt her stir a little in her sleep before she opened her eyes and focusing them on me and weakly smiled at me.

"Hi,"

"Hi," I replied through tears.

She lifted her hand and used the back of her hand and wiped my falling tears as best as she could making me laugh a little.

"Don't cry Keri," She whispered.

"I can't help it I thought I lost you Khloe," I admitted as the tears fell harder and I rubbed my hand across her face.

"But you didn't, I'm here," She spoke softly.

I stood up and walked to the nightstand and poured her some water and put a straw in it bringing it to her mouth for her to take some, after she was done I put it back down and looked at her.

"I'm going to call the doctor," I told her.

"Wait before you do I need you to know that I haven't been taking drugs, I promised you after the last time that I wouldn't do it anymore and I haven't Keri, I swear I haven't," She spoke on the verge of tears.

"Shhh, don't worry about it Khloe, I already know, it wasn't your fault," I tried to assure her.

"Then how did I get here?" She cried.

"It's a long story just know that I believe you," I smiled at her before I pressed the call nurse button.

While we waited for the nurse to come in the room I couldn't take my eyes off her, she was just so beautiful and to think I almost lost her behind the likes of someone as evil as Max. I know I had to make some major changes in my life to ensure that something like this never happens again.

"Hi, I'm doctor Illette," She walked in introducing herself.

"Hey you," I spoke.

"Dr. Anderson I didn't realize you were in here," She said with a smile.

"Yeah not working though this is my sister Khloe," I told her.

"Oh okay, well from the looks of all your test it looks like you were poisoned which explains your seizures and you coming in here unresponsive. If you didn't get here when you did you wouldn't be here today," She stated.

"POISIONED?" I yelled out shocked.

"Yes, from the look of her labs it looks like it's been happening for a little while now, but this last dose was just enough to cause her to pass out," She explained.

"Do you know what was used for the poison?" I questioned pissed off.

"That we couldn't tell, but we're flushing her system out now with the IV and hoping to get her back to normal soon as can be," She told us looking between the both of us.

"Okay great, thank you," I responded.

"When can I go home?" Khloe questioned.

"In a few days, we need to make sure your system is flushed and everything is back to normal before we let you go," She told her.

"Okay," She replied in a sad tone.

"Thanks Doctor," I smiled.

"No problem, do you ladies need anything else?" She asked.

"No, I think we're good here," I answered.

"Okay, if you need anything don't hesitate to call me," She smiled before walking out the room.

"You okay?" I asked rubbing her hair.

"Honestly, I don't know, but I'm going to take a nap," She spoke in a sad voice turning over in her bed.

I kicked off my shoes and got in the bed with my sister, she turned over and laid her head on my chest as I just held her and thought about how I was going to get Max back for what he did to me and my sister. I don't know what I was going to do but little did he know something was coming his way and it would be big.

Chapter 6- Cobain

I watched as Keri walked away and then turned my focus back on the doctor as he explained what was going on with Shyne's stupid ass.

"We were able to control the bleeding, but she did lose a lot of blood so we had to give her a transfusion. We were also able to get the bullet out with minimal damage to her organs, right now she's heavily sedated and will be in and out of it for a while, she can probably go home in about a week," He explained.

"Thank you, doctor, I really appreciate all that you did for her," I stated sincerely shaking his hand.

"No problem," He replied with a smile.

"Can I go see her?"

"Yeah right, this way," He responded leading me to her room.

Once I got to her room, I walked inside and just stared at her ass laying in the bed, I can't believe her ass really had the audacity to follow me and pull a gun on me and Keri. This shit wasn't sitting well with me, and if it wasn't for the fact that she was Kaylee's mom I would have let her ass die in front of Keri's house. I got to the foot of the bed and just looked at her with a look of distain; I can't believe something so beautiful could be so ugly and hateful on the inside.

"Wake up," I spoke slapping her on the leg making her moan out in pain.

"Ahh, Cobain" She moaned opening her eyes looking at me with fear in her eyes, she knew I didn't play disrespect at all and she crossed the line this time.

"Don't be scared now, you weren't scared when you had a gun pointed at me," I stated in a sinister tone of voice.

"I... I... I didn't mean for the gun to go off," She stuttered.

"What the fuck do you mean you didn't mean for the gun to go off? What the fuck do you think guns do when you point them with your hand on the got dam trigger Shyne?" I barked making her jump a little.

She looked at me as her eyes filled with tears, but that shit wasn't fazing me at all, she did this shit so now she was going to have to hear my mouth.

"Don't get scared now, what would make you pull a gun on me and think that I would be okay with that shit?"

"I'm sorry," She whispered.

"Huh, sorry, sorry got your ass in this dam hospital bed and since your ass was out here being a got dam private eye and pulling guns out on people like you the got dam police where the fuck is my daughter?" I shouted making the tears that's he was holding on to finally fall from her eyes.

"She's at Mickelle's house for a sleepover," She spoke as the tears fell.

"I'll be getting her tomorrow and she will be staying with me, even when you come home she will be with me because after the stunt you just pulled it kind of lets me know that you're a little unfit. So, when I feel like your back to your old self I'll think about letting her come back home with you," I explained.

"No, you can't take my baby from me, she's all I have," She cried.

"You should have thought about all that while you were on your mission impossible shit," I shrugged.

"I'm sorry, but what do you want me to say. You NEVER took me serious, Cobain I love you, I've been in love with you since I first laid eyes on you and all you did was fuck me. I tried to be there for you, never nagged you at all, did any and everything you asked of me and for what just to get your ass to kiss. I thought maybe just maybe when you found out I was pregnant that it would change and you would be the man that I know you could be, but nope that didn't even work," She cried.

I felt kind of bad but then I didn't, she knew the kind of man I was when we first started fuckin' around.

"Listen you knew the kind of nigga I was when we first met, I told you I wasn't looking for anything serious but you still chose to stick and try and change a nigga, to keep it perfectly real with you I don't even know how you even ended up pregnant because I always strapped up but that's neither here nor there I love baby girl and wouldn't change shit now. YOU stayed when you didn't have to so don't get mad at me because you didn't get the results YOU were hoping for," I explained.

"Why don't you love me?" She asked still crying.

"SHYNE STAY FOCUSED, what if you succeeded in killing yourself or me what about Kaylee? Did you think about her at all while you were holding that gun on me?" I asked.

"OF COURSE, I WAS this was all for her. She deserves a happy family a mother and father that love her and live together," She yelled making her machines go off.

"Listen calm down before you hurt yourself," I spoke looking at the machines.

I walked over and got her some water for her so she could try and relax.

"I'm going to get up on out of here, I'll be back to check on you in a few days," I told her.

"Can you bring Kaylee up here please?" She asked.

"Hell no, she just saw me in the hospital and now you, nah she doesn't need to see you in here. You can see her when you come home, I'll tell her you went away for a few days," I stated.

She nodded her head up and down even though I know she wasn't pleased with what I just said but I really didn't give a fuck. I walked towards the door then stopped.

"Next time you pull a gun on me I'll forget your Kaylee's mom and kill you dead," I threatened and walked out the room.

I walked up to the nurse's station and asked for Keri's sister's room, I wanted to see if Keri was going to leave with me. Once I had what I needed I went to the elevator and got on and made my way to Khloe's room. When I got there, I knocked and waited until I heard someone, when I didn't I slowly pushed open the door and stuck my head inside and saw Keri asleep with her sister in the bed.

I quietly walked over to the bed and tapped Keri, she stirred lightly in her sleep but didn't wake up. I knew she said she was tired so I felt kind of bad waking her up now.

"Keri," I called out in a whisper while I tapped her leg again making her eyes open.

She looked around then focused on me then looked down at her sister who was sleeping peacefully on her.

"You want to get out of here?" I asked.

She nodded her head and slowly got out the bed trying her best not to wake her sister, this was my first time seeing her sister and she and Keri were basically twins it was crazy. She managed to get out the bed and kissed her on the forehead before covering her up with the blanket.

I grabbed her hand and pulled her into me kissing her on the top of her head, I put my arm over her shoulder and we walked out the hospital room together.

***

We got to my house and I let her have my room and I took the guest room only because I knew that I had one of the best mattresses ever and I know she was tired and probably in pain so I wanted her to have a great sleep even if for one night.

"There's towels and washcloths in the closet in the bathroom," I told her as I walked in the bedroom.

"Thank you," She replied with a smile.

I walked over to my dresser and pulled out a shirt and boxers and handed them to her before getting some out for myself along with a pair of basketball shorts.

"Everything you need is in the bathroom, I don't know if I have any of that girly stuff y'all ladies like to bathe with but you can check on the lower shelf in the bathroom," I told her making her cut her eyes at me.

"Why would you have girly stuff in your bathroom?" She asked.

"My mom stays here sometimes and just how I'm giving you my room, I do the same for her," I admitted making her blush.

"Oh," Was all she could say making me laugh.

"Don't oh me now doc, let me find out I got you feeling some type of way," I chuckled making her blush harder.

"Anyway, let me go shower, thank you again," She smiled walking into the bathroom ignoring my statement.

I laughed and walked out the room and headed to the guestroom so I could shower and get some rest because I just know tomorrow is going to be a long day. I pulled out my phone and called Ali up to see what his progress was.

"YO, any luck tonight?"

"Nah not really, I found the place that they took her to but when I got there the place was empty," He explained.

"How the hell you find it?" I asked.

That's when he explained to me that he basically broke into her job and got the info that he needed. This nigga was a beast and didn't give no fucks about shit when he was on a mission, he was going to get shit done.

"Damn bro so what now?" I asked sitting on the bed.

"I put in a few calls to locate this nigga family, he thinks he got one up on me but nah I got a trick for his ass," He stated.

"I feel you bro, just keep me posted, I'll be out with you tomorrow after I make sure the doc is good," I told him.

"Ight cool," He replied hanging up.

I tossed the phone on the bed and walked into the adjoining bathroom to shower, a nigga was beat and ready to take it the fuck down. I stripped out of my clothes and turned on the shower, once it was at the right temperature I got in and placed my hand on the wall as I stood under the water letting it fall over me.

I grabbed my rag and my Tom Ford body wash and washed my body down, I made sure to shampoo my beard as well. Once I was done I rinsed off and got out the shower, I wrapped the towel around my waist and finished taking care of my hygiene. After that was done I walked out the bathroom and sat on my bed and put my head in my hands and just took a deep breath.

I grabbed my clothes and threw them on and forgot that I left my slippers in my bedroom, I stood up and walked out the room and headed to my room. I knocked and waited for Keri to say something. When I didn't get a response, I walked in and went straight to the closet for my slippers. I grabbed them and walked out the closet and right into Keri causing her to drop the towel.

"I'm sorry ma, I thought I had time to grab my stuff before you came out the bathroom," I admitted looking over her body and getting myself worked up.

She quickly picked up her towel and covered her body but the damage was already done I saw the bruising on her body. I didn't even say shit else I just walked out the room slamming the door behind me. I went downstairs to my bar and took a shot of something strong, the way my anger was building up right now a nigga was needing this right now.

When I catch that pussy ass nigga I was going to kill him with my bare hands, her beautiful body with all those scars and bruises new and old. I couldn't imagine my daughter going through all of that by the hands of another man. I would be doing life in jail behind her. I took another shot then went upstairs to my room that I was crashing in for the night.

I closed my door and hit my lights and got into bed, I cut the TV on and turned the volume down low and laid there and hoped sleep came to me soon.

KNOCK… KNOCK

"Come in," I spoke.

The door opens and in walks Keri, the light from the television bounced off her face and I saw that she was looking a little down. I sat up in the bed and turned my lamp on before I looked at her.

"What's up doc?" I asked.

"About what you saw back there," She started to explain before I cut her off.

"No need to go into detail, I'm good on that," I admitted.

"Okay," She replied in a whisper.

"Don't look like that; I'm just keeping it real with you. I'm trying to forget what I saw and if you bring it up again I'm going to get all upset again and we don't need that," I stated truthfully.

"Understood," She spoke about to turn to leave.

"Doc," I called out before she left.

"Yes," She responded.

"Come lay with me," I caught myself saying.

She turned and faced me unsure of what she should do next. She bit her bottom lip and twiddled her thumbs lie a little kid making me chuckle out loud.

"I only ask once, if you don't want to its cool, close the door on your way out," I told her leaning over and cutting my lamp off before laying back down.

I wasn't about to play with her I was tired and those two shots I took were starting to creep on me. After a few second's I felt the other side of my bed get lower and I felt Keri behind me. I turned over and pulled her on me where she rested her head on my chest, she fit so perfectly in my arms. This shit just felt to perfect that a nigga was low key nervous to even be feeling like this.

Shit like this was new to me and I wasn't really sure what to make of this, but I was feeling her and I was going to do whatever I needed to do to make sure I didn't lose her.

"Thank you," I heard her softly say bringing me from my thoughts.

Instead of responding I kissed the top of her forehead and fell asleep with her in my arms, I could definitely get used to this every night.

Chapter 7- Cree

I was sitting in this place for what seem like forever and they had me in my bra and panties feeding me scraps of food, and sips of water whenever they felt like they wanted to come down and be nice according to them. They had a pail under the chair for me to go to the bathroom in, I have never felt so disrespected in my life, when I get out of here I was putting some distance between Ali and myself. I have been beaten and if I would have stuck to my guns and ignored him like I said I was going to I wouldn't be here right now.

"You are really beautiful," The creepy man spoke looking at me with lust in his eyes.

I closed my eyes and tried my best to ignore him as long as I possibly could until I felt his breath on my neck.

"What the fuck do you want?" I asked through gritted teeth.

"I want you," He replied licking me on my ear causing me to cringe.

He started to untie my hands as he had this crazed look in his eye, making me nervous.

"If you try anything slick I will kill you and say you tried to escape," He threatened.

He started to untie me and my mind already started to race on how I was going to try to escape. I was feeling weak as hell but I would have found a way out of here, even if I had to die trying. From the look he was giving me I already knew what he was thinking and I wasn't even about to go out this way. He picked me up and placed me on the mattress that was in the corner of the room.

I backed up against the wall as fast as I could, I looked around the room trying to find something I could use for a weapon, when I couldn't find one my eyes went back on the guy and he already had his pants down and was pulling his shirt over his head. He looked at me and then grabbed me by the legs and pulled me closer to him.

"AHHHHH NOOOOOOOO, LET ME GO," I yelled trying to fight him off.

I managed to kick him in his dick and scramble to off the bed, I almost made it to the steps until he grabbed me by the leg making me fall and hit my head on the ground.

"Ahhhh," I yelled out in pain.

My head was pounding from the fall but that didn't stop me from trying to still fight him, I managed to hit him in the mouth making him look down at me and slap me making me see stars.

"Stop fighting me," He yelled as he wrapped his hand around my neck.

I didn't even have any more fight left in me. I was so dazed from the fall and slap that I just laid there as he ripped my panties off me.

"Please don't," I moaned out in pain.

"Shut up, I know you want this, I saw how you been looking at me," He groaned as he got on top of me trying to spread my legs apart.

"NOOOOOOOO, STOPPPPP," I yelled out.

As soon as I felt his hard dick on the outside of my pussy, I started screaming and fighting as loud and as much as I could pushing through the pain I was currently experiencing. The next thing I know I heard a gun click behind his dead, I opened my eyes and saw Dee the man who originally kidnapped me with a look on his face that I couldn't read.

"WHAT THE FUCK DO YOU THINK YOU ARE DOING?" He asked through gritted teeth casing the man to freeze up.

"I'm… I'm… not doing shit boss," He stuttered.

"Really it don't look like nothing nigga. Get the fuck up," He spoke gun butting him in the back of the head.

He got off and stood there with his dick swinging and head down embarrassed that he got caught in this situation.

"Is this what I pay you to do?" He questioned tilting his head to the side with the gun still aimed at him.

"No boss," He replied.

'I didn't think so," He responded putting a bullet straight through his eyes.

"AHHHHHHH," I yelled wiping the blood from my face.

I screamed out as I watched his body drop right in front of me, Dee looked at me and grabbed the handkerchief from his suit and tossed it to me.

"Clean your face," He spoke.

I grabbed it off the bed and wiped the blood splatter off my face as he stood there and watched.

"I know I have you here against your will and have beaten you but one thing I don't condone is rape which is why I killed him," He admitted.

I just looked at him, I didn't know how to take what he just said. How are you a bad guy but have limitations on what you can and won't do?

"I'll get someone down here to clean this mess up so you won't have to look at this while you're down here," He explained turning to walk away.

I looked around and tried to see if I could find anything here to use to try to escape with when he leaves, then I noticed him stop.

"If you think about trying anything, I promise I will kill you dead," He said no even bothering to look back at me as he made his way out the basement leaving me sitting there scared.

Chapter 8- Ali

This nigga dragon thought his shit was safe because couldn't anyone find his family, but everyone was traceable for the right price. So I found this nigga family all hidden in a whole other state, so I sent my people out there and I was currently on my way there myself because I had to make sure shit got done the right way. I know Cobain was busy with Keri so I was sitting him out with this one until I really needed him for the action.

I hopped on the private jet that I had waiting for me so that I could take this trip to Arizona, like who the fuck really lives out in these places. All I could think about was that episode of Martin where that little kid was like *"I'm sorry Martin I just didn't wanna go to Arizona"* that's how I was feeling at this moment but I knew I had business to attend to. I needed my shorty back home with me and wasn't going to rest until she was back where she belonged.

I just knew this 5-hour flight was about to be long as hell, so I was about to get some rest until it was time for us to land because it was about to be straight nonstop action and I had to be on point. I had all my guns loaded and ready for action, I already had a few tricks up my sleeve that was going to guarantee a reaction from that nigga and make that nigga hand over Cree. It all brought a smile to my face just thinking about it.

***

I pulled up to the address that my mans had sent me, I put my gloves on and put the silencer on my gun and got out the car. I wasn't trying to be beating around the bush, I needed shit to be done and over with just as fast as it started.

Knock... Knock...

"Who is it?" I heard a lady call out from behind the door.

I didn't respond because this is the type of neighborhood where they were still going to open the door even if you didn't say anything. I heard the locks unlocking and smiled to myself.

"Hi, can I help you?" A sexy lady answered the door, she put me in the mindset of Meghan Good but just a little bit older still fine as fuck no doubt.

"I'm a friend of your husbands and I came to talk to him," I smiled.

"Oh I don't know if you spoke to him recently or not but he's out of town, and won't be back for a little while," She told me.

"Oh, I didn't know," I faked.

"Yeah, I'm sorry you had to come all the way out here for nothing," She replied with a genuine smile, making me feel a little bad that I was about to fuck up her day.

Welp her nigga didn't give a fuck about my day when his ass snatched Cree, so I was about to havoc hell on everything and everyone.

"It's cool. Do you mind if I use the bathroom before I get back on the road?"

"Um, I'm not really sure if that will be a good idea," She admitted.

"I'll be fast, in and out,"

"Okay... I guess that's okay," She spoke in an unsure tone as she opened the door further letting me in.

I walked in as she closed the door and as soon as she turned to face me my gun was in her face.

"AHHHHHHH," She yelled.

"Shut the fuck up and walk to the living room and have a seat before I blow your damn head off," I threatened as she led me to the living room.

"Please what do you want? We have money is that what you want, I can get it for you," She cried as she sat down.

"Man don't nobody want your damn money, your nigga has something that belongs to me and I need it back and if I don't get it back you will die," I told her shrugging my shoulders.

"What does he have?" She asked.

"Who is here with you?" I asked looking around.

"The kids are down for a nap and my mom is in the pool out back," She responded.

I didn't think the kids were home but fuck it, maybe that will get shit moving a little faster.

"This is what I'm going to need for you to do, go get everyone then bring them inside, and then we are going to call your husband," I stated.

"Okay,"

"Good, let's go," I told her.

I stood to the side and saw her grab for something and before I knew it she was getting a shot off missing me and entering the wall causing me to shoot her in the shoulder.

"AHHHHHHHHH" She cried out in pain.

"I see your man has you trained well, as he should, not trained well enough though which is why you over here bleeding and shit stupid. Suck that shit up and let's go," I said poppin' her in the back of her head with my free hand.

"Wait put this on," I told her tossing her a sweater. I don't care if it was the middle of summer shorty shouldn't have tried to blast me and she wouldn't be bleeding right now.

We walked upstairs first and walked into the kid's bedroom where they were sleeping peacefully.

"Danica and Derrick wake up," She spoke shaking the kids.

The little girl woke up and rubbed her eyes and just stared at me, with a confused look. The little boy was just like a nigga and wouldn't wake up at first.

"Derrick baby, it's time to get up."

He finally woke up and looked over at me with this evil ass look, and I already knew he was about to be a douche.

"Who you?" He asked when he finally got his bearings together

"I'm your uncle Ali," I replied.

"How you my uncle and I don't even know you?" He questioned.

"Don't worry about all that little nigga, let's go downstairs like your mama said,"

He looked up at his mom and she smiled weakly and nodded her head then he got up and we all went downstairs. He kept looking back at me trying to figure out who I really was, but I didn't give a fuck as long as he didn't jump bad like his mama I wasn't going to have to handle him. I hated a bad ass kid.

They all sat in the living room and were up under their mom, confused.

"Call your husband," I told her.

Soon as she was about to reply I heard a lady in the kitchen.

"Tiffany, I have lunch ready," She yelled out.

She looked up at me not sure what to say, I mouthed her to what to say.

"Bring it in here ma, I'll get the kids," She replied.

"Okay, I'm coming,"

We heard footsteps coming and as soon as she got to the living room she dropped the tray and started screaming then tried to run. I chased her down and grabbed her by her thin ass ponytail causing her to fall on her back. I pointed the gun in her face and dared her to scream again.

"Get up slowly and take your ass in the dam living room," I spoke through gritted teeth.

She slowly got up as best she could and walked into the living room sitting next to her daughter looking scared as fuck.

"Like I was saying, call your fuckin husband NOW," I yelled getting impatient.

She picked up the phone and called her husband looking scared shitless.

"Put it on speaker,"

"Hey babe, I'm a little busy right now and can't talk, what's up," He answered soon as he picked up the phone.

"Ba… babe," She responded.

"What's wrong Tiff why you sound like that?" He asked sounding concerned.

"What's up you punk motherfucker," I greeted.

"If you touch my family,-"

"YOU WILL WHAT? NOTHING! LOOKS LIKE I'M CALLING THE SHOTS NOW STUPID MOTHER FUCKER! IF YOU DON'T WANT YOUR BEAUTIFUL FAMILY HERE TO DIE, I SUGGEST YOU MEET ME WITH CREE OR YOU WILL BE HAVING A FUNERAL FOR YOUR WHOLE FAMILY WITH NO BODIES," I threatened.

It was silent on the other end of the phone for a minute until I finally heard him talk.

"What do you want?" He asked in a defeated tone.

"Man quit acting dumb as fuck, you know what I want," I barked getting annoyed,

"When and where?"

"Now it's when and where because I have your family how about I just shoot your wife right now for even making me go through all of this in the first place,"

"Let's not get dramatic now,"

"You have yet to see dramatic," I replied hanging up the phone.

"What are you going to do with us?" The grandmother asked.

"I haven't decided yet, but let's go," I stated.

"She doesn't look to well, what's wrong with her?" The old bat asked.

"She got shot that's what's wrong with her dumb ass," I stated pushing them out the house.

"She needs to see a doctor," She pleaded.

"I'll think about it,"

I made them all get into the awaiting van that I had on the side of the house, once they were all inside and pulling off we stopped down the block and I turned and watched as the house exploded.

"OH MY GOD," They all yelled out.

"Let's go," I ordered the driver.

He pulled off and made his way back to the air strip taking me back home, I was ready to get out of this dam state.

Chapter 9- Keri

I woke up feeling so refreshed, I haven't slept this good in so long. I rolled over and saw that Cobain was still sleeping and I couldn't help but to stare at him. He was such a handsome man, built in all the right places and his beard was trimmed to perfect this man was just so beautiful and I felt lucky to be in his presence.

I laid down and just basked in this moment afraid that it would come to an end soon and I would have to go back to the real world where all my issues were still waiting for me.

"You been up long?" Cobain asked still with his eyes closed.

"How did you know I was up?" I questioned.

"I don't sleep hard and I felt you moving around," He admitted to me finally opening his eyes and looking over at me.

"I see, sorry if I woke you,"

"Nah you good, I needed to get up anyway," He stated sitting up in the bed looking at me with a smirk.

"Why you looking at me like that?" I asked blushing.

"You are even beautiful when you wake up, despite the morning breath," He joked.

"Oh my god, shut up," I laughed covering my mouth.

"It's cool baby girl, I know you couldn't be all perfect," He laughed getting out the bed.

He walked out the room and a few seconds later came back with a spare toothbrush for me.

"Here you go doc, go handle your business," He spoke handing me the toothbrush.

"Thank you," I replied still covering my mouth walking into the bathroom.

I closed the door behind me and turned on the water and just looked at my reflection in the mirror, for the first time in a while I didn't look tired or worn out, I wasn't looking at bruises on my body trying to figure out how I was going to have to cover them up. I was actually happy to be up and alive and that's just after one night of being with Cobain.

I brushed my teeth then washed my face and walked out the bathroom to see Cobain, sitting on the bed texting on his phone. I don't know why a hint of jealousy shot through my veins when he wasn't even my man.

"Fix your face doc, I'm texting Ali," He laughed.

"I don't know what you're talking about," I lied.

"Yeah okay, sure you don't," He chuckled getting up off the bed and walking towards me.

"What are your plans for the day?" I questioned as he stood in my face.

"Well after we have breakfast, I need to run and meet Ali then pick up my princess," He told me.

"Oh okay," I said kind of bummed.

"You're more than welcome to come back later after your done with whatever your day consist of you doing," He suggested leaning in and kissing me on the lips.

He had the softest lips ever, he kissed me with such passion that it made my knees buckle. I had to grab a hold of him or I swear that I would have fallen down. He slowly pulled away and looked me in the eyes with a smirk on his face.

"I'll keep that in mind," I replied with a lusty look in my eyes.

"I know," He cockily spoke.

"Whatever," I laughed picking up the pillow and throwing it at him which of course he caught and threw it right back.

"Don't start nothing you can't finish doc," He laughed.

"Just an FYI anything I start, I most definitely can finish," I stated seductively looking him in the eyes.

"Oh, is that right?" He responded licking his lips.

"It is," I stated in a matter of fact tone.

He placed his hand on my chin and raised my face to look him in the eyes, then leaned down and kissed me again. Then picked me up as I wrapped my legs around his waist and he guided me to the bed. He laid me down on the bed without breaking our kiss, he pulled down my shorts with his hands then slid his finger inside my pussy making me arch my back.

"Shiiiiiiiiiittttttttt," I moaned out in pleasure.

He continued to move his finger around getting me wetter and wetter, he focused on my spot instantly making me cum.

"Ahhhhhh fuckkkkk,"

Once I came he pulled his finger out and licked my, cum off his fingers, and looked at me.

"Damn doc, I could get use to eating you. You taste good as fuck," He stated.

I rolled my eyes and watched him as he stood up and pulled his shorts off, my eyes went straight to his dick and my eyes damn near jumped out the socket.

"Don't get nervous doc," He smirked.

"Shut up, please," I replied rolling my eyes.

He got back on the bed on top of me and kissed me again as he placed the head of his dick at the opening of my pussy. I swear my breathing got shallow as he slowly started to enter me.

"Shit doc," He groaned as he finally made it in.

"Mmmmmm,"

He didn't move right away, he opened his eyes and looked me straight in mine and stared into my eyes as he started slowly moving inside.

"Ssssss oh shit, Cobain," I moaned out.

The way he was making my body feel right now was out of this world, he was taking his time, making sure I felt every inch of him inside of me.

"Fuckkkkkkkk, you feel soooooo good," I yelled.

"This pussy is so wet doc," He groaned into my ear.

I lifted my leg giving him more access inside of me as he continued to assault my pussy, the hurting he was doing was so damn good.

"Ohhhhhhhh myyyyyyy gooooooodddd," I shouted as I stuck my nails further in his back.

The next thing I know he was flipping me over on my stomach and inserting his dick in me from the back.

"Shitttttttttttt," I panted.

"Fuck doc,"

He had one hand on my waist and the other on my neck as pounded me from the back making me cum back to back.

"That's right doc cum on this dick," He said through gritted teeth.

"I can't take it anymoreeeeeeeee," I screamed through labored breathes.

"Shit I'm 'bout to cum,"

He put his other hand on my waist and held on as he pumped inside of me, I felt his dick getting harder inside of me then after a few more pumps I felt him release inside of me.

"AHHHHHHHHHH, SHITTTTTT," He groaned then slapped my ass before pulling out and falling on the bed next to me.

We both laid there trying to catch our breaths and didn't say anything to each other.

"If you hold out from me again I think I'm going to have to kill you," Cobain spoke breaking the silence and making me laugh.

"Your such an asshole," I replied slapping him on his arm.

"I'm serious doc that shit right there babyyyyyyy, is the real deal,"

"Whatever," I laughed.

"So now what doc?" He asked looking over at me.

"Honestly, I don't know, I just need to figure my life out before I bring you into it, it's not fair to involve you in my drama," I told him honestly.

"I hear you, I'm about to make a phone call, I'll meet you downstairs," He responded getting up from the bed.

"Okay," I spoke in a soft voice.

"Make yourself at home, Mi Casa Es Su Casa," He joked walking out the room.

"I always wanted a bilingual man," I laughed back getting off the bed and making my way downstairs to the kitchen.

I walked down the steps to the kitchen, his house was decorated so beautifully. I admired every piece of art work that was here and the colors of his house went so well together, he had some good taste. After touring the house, I finally found my way to the kitchen which was even more beautiful.

The smoke grey walls with white trims was everything and was giving me ideas for my new place. I just couldn't wait to start over with my new life, just Khloe and myself. I walked to the coffee pot and rinsed it then grabbed the coffee off the counter and added it to the filter and waited for it to brew.

I sat at the island and waited for Cobain to come down and join me, I still don't know what it was about him that kept drawing me to him, but I wasn't mad at it either.

"I see you found the coffee okay," He announced as he walked into the kitchen.

"I did," I smiled looking at him.

"Well let me whip something up for us real quick," He stated pulling out a pan.

"Let me find out you on your Chef Boy R Dee shit," I laughed.

"Nah I'm more on my Chef Boy R Cee shit. I can't do much but I can scramble the fuck out of some eggs though," He admitted as he walked to the refrigerator.

"I guess it's a good thing I love eggs huh?" I laughed.

"Well you about to really love me then because when I tell you I be putting my foot in these eggs,"

"I can't wait," I smiled.

I watched as he made his way around the kitchen doing his thing as we had little conversation. This shit was just so easy for him and I was having a great time talking to him and watching him in his element.

"Voila," He said placing a plate of eggs in front of me along with a cup of coffee.

"This looks and smells so good, you even give great presentation," I smirked.

"Well you know I told you I had skills," He chuckled while licking his lips.

He placed a plate down for him and went to the fridge and poured himself a glass of orange juice then sat down across from me.

"Bon Appétit,"

I smiled and placed my fork in my eggs and, placed some in my mouth. I closed my eyes and savored the taste.

"I take it that you like them?"

"These are some of the best eggs I've had in my life," I admitted.

"Thank you,"

"I don't get it I watched you make these eggs and you make them exactly like I do but they taste different, so I don't get it," I told him with a confused look as I continued to eat the eggs.

"When you weren't looking I added my secret ingredient,"

"What was it?" I asked.

"If I tell you I'll have to kill you," He told me seriously before he busted out laughing.

"Whatever," I replied rolling my eyes.

"I'm just kidding, I can't tell you though, but when I do that means I trust you,"

The rest of the time we ate we talked and got to know each other a little more, it was so easy talking to him.

"Doc I want to ask you something and I don't want you to lie to me," He said looking at me seriously.

I looked up at him and swallowed my food hard and nodded, I took a sip of my coffee and waited for him to ask his question.

"Why do you stay with Max when he abuses you?" He questioned with a serious look on his face.

I put my head down embarrassed about my situation, how could I explain to him that I always put people ahead of me and I did what I had to do to make sure my sister was forever good.

"Cat got your tongue doc?"

"Um no it's not that, I'm just trying to find the words to explain," I said truthfully.

"Take your time,"

"It's like this… have you ever had someone depend on you to the point that you would do anything for them to make sure that they needed or wanted for anything no matter what the consequence is for you?" I questioned looking him straight in the eyes.

"Actually, I have anything I've done was to make sure my daughter was taken care of," He stated in a matter of fact tone.

"Well that's my situation, my sister depends on me and no matter what I have to do, to keep her safe and alive I'll do it. Simple," I spoke before bringing my coffee mug to my lips.

"So, you being a punching bag is keeping her safe?"

"Actually, it is," I responded placing the last bite of eggs in my mouth.

"Please help me understand doc, because shit isn't adding up with me," He spoke in an aggravated tone of voice.

I took a deep breath and started telling him all about me and Max from the beginning leaving nothing out. He wanted to know why I did what I did and what made me put up with the shit I did so I told him. By the time I was done I didn't even realize that I was crying. Cobain handed me a tissue so I could wipe my eyes.

"Thank you," I spoke with a weak smile.

"Don't cry doc,"

"I can't help it, but do you see why I have to do what I do, my sister depends on me and I will do whatever I have to do to make sure I don't let her down again," I cried.

"To me it seems like you are carrying around alot of guilt that you don't need to," He finally spoke up.

"Maybe I am, who knows but I know I can't lose my sister,"

"I understand that but you going about shit the wrong way, let me help you Keri," He suggested as he lifted my head to face him.

"I can't, I need to do this on my own. I will never give another man the power over me again. My sister is my responsibility and that's how it will stay, thank you but no thank you," I stated getting up and placing my plate in the sink.

"First off let's get one thing straight, I am not that punk mother fucker so don't ever in your life try and compare me to him," He told me pissed off.

"I'm not saying that you are but,"

"But what Keri? I have a daughter and if she even went through half of what you have I would kill that nigga dead. Have you seen your body? Like really seen your body doc? You have an amazing body but I'm sure it would look a lot better without all them bruises on it," He jabbed at me.

"You know what, FUCK YOU COBAIN," I yelled walking away.

"Doc," He called out but I wasn't trying to hear what the fuck he was trying to say.

I made it up to his room and grabbed my clothes and started putting them back on before he even made it upstairs.

"KERI,"

I realized he only called me Keri when he wanted to get my attention any other time it was doc, if it was any other time I would have acknowledged it but right now I was pissed and had nothing to say to him at all, I was leaving his house and him alone.

"I know you hear me calling you,"

"I know you see me ignoring you also," I replied pulling my shirt over my head.

"I didn't mean it like that," He tried to explain.

"I know Cobain, its cool," I responded with a fake smile.

"It's not it came out wrong,"

"No, it came out perfectly fine and its okay, don't you think I see my scars every time I look in the mirror, do you think I asked for this? Because I didn't, I use to be so proud of my body but now when I look in the mirror I cry at what I see,"

"Doc,"

"Don't, I get it; I was stupid for staying with him. I know but at that time I had no other options, so I played the hand that I was dealt," I cried walking out leaving him behind.

I got down the stairs and was about to leave when I remembered that he drove me here, I quickly searched for a pair of keys to one of his cars. I found a pair in a bowl near the front door, I quickly picked them up and ran out the house. I hit the alarm until I found the car that it belonged to, and I jumped inside and pulled off without looking back. I felt my phone vibrate and when I picked it up I saw it was a text from Cobain.

Cobain: I get that your mad but don't forget you got a nigga here waiting for you

I didn't even bother to respond because he clearly didn't know who the fuck I was but I was surely about to show him how my block game works.

Chapter 10- Max

I've been in this hotel drinking my life away since the night I left the house after beating Keri. I know this last time I really fucked up, but seeing her with that other man drove me insane. She was supposed to be my fiancé but she was out living life like she was a teenager without a care in the world. That's when I knew I had to do something to get her back, whenever Khloe was sick Keri did any and everything I asked of her to make sure she got the help she needed.

Now don't get me wrong I loved the fuck out of Keri, and I still plan on making her my wife whether she likes it or not. Her mom and I had a deal, and I planned on making sure she kept up her end of the bargain. I invested a lot of money into this and planned on getting my money's worth.

Knock…Knock

"Who is it?" I called out.

"It's me Bernadette."

I got up from the couch and went and opened the door and just stared at the woman on the other end.

"Well are you going to stand there and look at me or you going to let me in?" She asked placing her hand on her hip.

I stood to the side and widened the door allowing her access to my hotel room, closing the door behind her.

"You look like shit, and you stink," She acknowledged turning her face up at me.

"Yeah well, I've seen better days," I admitted.

"Why did you call me here Max? I have better shit to do with my time then sit here in your face and watch you sulk. As a matter of fact why are you here in this hotel and not at home with my daughter?" She questioned.

"Something happened."

"What happened Max?" She asked looking at me suspiciously.

"Well what the fuck happened?" She yelled.

"I beat Keri."

"Okay, you always beat her. What was so different this time?" She inquired crossing her arms across her chest.

I told her how I went off and beat her ass like she was my child. I told her that I beat her so bad that I thought I killed her.

"YOU DID WHAT?"

"I know, I didn't mean for it to get that bad," I admitted.

"You, stupid prick, where the fuck is she at?"

"I don't know, when I was done I just walked out leaving her on the floor and coming straight here," I explained.

Whap...

She slapped the fuck out of me making me taste my own blood.

"You busted my lip you crazy bat."

"You lucky that's all I did, whipping my daughter like you don't have no damn sense. What the fuck is wrong with you?" She asked pacing the floor.

"Please don't act like you give a fuck now, cut the mother Theresa act. That ship has sailed long time ago," I told her.

"Shut the fuck up, just because I let you hit my daughter doesn't mean that I don't love her," She tried to tell me.

"You sure do have a fucked up way of showing your love," I stated looking at her sideways.

"Whatever, I gave her to you basically on a silver platter and you just had to go and fuck it up for all of us."

"It's still time, I'm going to get her back," I stated.

"How?" She asked looking at me crazy.

"I'll figure it out, but what I need from you is to talk to her and see where her head is at."

"I'll see what I can do," She replied shaking her head at me.

"What made you flip out this time?"

I told her about me having her followed and how she was cheating with another man. I left out the part about me keeping

Khloe sick, because then she would have really lost it. For some strange reason, she loved Khloe more then she loved Keri, it was kind of weird, but I think it had something to do with their daddies.

"She probably getting sick of your shit. I'm actually surprised she stayed around this damn long," She acknowledged making me look at her sideways.

"What the fuck does that mean?"

"Nothing I'll give her a call later and see what's she up to, for this little stunt you going to have to come out your pocket more." She stated.

I looked at her like she was fuckin' stupid. I can't believe she cared more about the money then her own kid's wellbeing. I never understood mothers like that, she was the worst kind of mothers its even shocking that Keri came out the way she did with a mother like this to raise her.

"Yeah whatever just make sure she's back home by the time I get there," I told her opening the door for her to get the hint that I wanted her gone.

"Don't be such a grouch, get yourself cleaned up and look like somebody worth loving again," She laughed her way out the door.

I slammed the door and looked around my hotel room. It was a complete mess, but at this moment I didn't care. I walked to the bar and poured myself another drink and drank it all then sat on my bed and waited until I got that call to go get my fiancé back.

Chapter 11- Cobain

Soon as Keri left I felt like shit, but then not really because she needed to hear the truth. I wanted to go after her but I was going to give her some time to cool off. I didn't know where she was going but it didn't matter because all my cars had trackers on them for personal reasons. I walked into my closet and grabbed me something to wear so I could get my day started.

Once I was dressed, I grabbed my phone and keys and was out the door. I jumped in my Range Rover sport and was on my way to pick up my pretty princess from her friend's house. I knew she was going to want to hang out with daddy all day since she hasn't seen me in a few days and that is exactly what I needed. I sent a text to her cell letting her know that I was on my way and to get ready.

I was going to have a daddy daughter day then drop her to my mom's house so I could bust this move with Ali later. A few minutes later, I pulled up to her friend house and sent her a text that I was outside. I sat back and waited for her to come to the car.

"Dadddyyyyyy," I heard Kaylee screaming.

I got out the car and walked to the other side and watched as she ran down the driveway straight towards me jumping into my arms.

"Hi baby girl, I missed you," I told her squeezing her tight.

"I missed you too daddy," She replied kissing me on the cheek.

"Hello Mr. Wade," The woman spoke with a seductive smile on her face. I already knew how this was going to go.

"Wassup Mrs.- "

"It's Ms. Jones, my husband and I separated a little while ago.

"I'm sorry to hear that," I replied looking her up and down.

Shorty was bad as fuck and I wouldn't mind taking her down pre-Keri days, but right now I couldn't see myself doing that.

"Don't be I'm glad," She said winking at me.

"I hear you, well thanks for keeping Kaylee, I appreciate it."

"Oh, it's not a problem we love having her here, she's so well behaved," She praised rubbing on my shoulder.

"Thank you, we try are best with her," I acknowledged, looking down at Kaylee with a smile.

"She's welcome over here anytime she wants to come. You are welcome to come with her as well," She winked making me chuckle.

"I'll keep that in mind, Kaylee let's go,"

I opened the door for Kaylee to get inside then walked around to the driver's side and got in the car. I looked back over at her friend's mom and her eyes never left me as she continued to bite her bottom lip. I put the car in park and hit the horn one time before pulling off.

"Daddy, Mrs. Jones wants you," Kaylee said as soon as we pulled off.

"What? How do you know that?" I asked laughing.

"Because when I told her you were coming she jumped up and changed her bra and fixed her makeup," She explained making me laugh at the silly shit.

"Oh really?"

"Yes daddy, I heard her tell her friend that she was going to try and make you hers," She told me rolling her eyes.

"Well you already know that you're my leading lady, right?" I asked looking at her through my rearview mirror.

"Of course, daddy," She replied with a bright smile on her face.

"Good."

"Where's mommy? I thought she was going to come get me?" She questioned.

"Mommy's stupid ass is in the hospital for shooting herself," I mumbled.

"Huh daddy?" She looked at me.

"I said mommy went out of town for a few days, so it's just going to be you and me," I spoke a little louder for her to hear me.

"Yaayyyyyyyyyy," She squealed from the backseat.

"I knew you would like that," I smiled.

"Heck yeah," She replied excitedly.

All I could do was laugh at my child, she was definitely all me and I couldn't be any prouder. She was the love of my life and I would move hell and high water for her. As much as I couldn't stand Shyne, I love the fact that she gave me my first-born daughter. I never knew what true love was until the day she was born. The love between Kaylee and I was a love that only real fathers would understand.

"So where are we going first daddy?" She asked breaking me from my thoughts.

"Where ever you wanna go baby girl,"

"Can we go to the mall daddy, I need to go to Claire's and get some new accessories pleaseeeeeeeeee," She pleaded.

I looked through my rearview and looked at her pouting at me and holding her hands together like she was begging.

"Okay you big brat,"

"Yaaaaaay, you're the best daddy ever," She clapped.

"I better be," I smirked at her.

I put the music on blast as we made our way to the mall, so she could put a dent in my pocket.

***

I don't know how I was conned into spending almost five hundred dollars in that little ass store. I swear she bought everything that the store had in every damn color, shit didn't make no damn sense. I ended up buying her a couple of pairs of kicks and a few outfits also along with a shitload of toys that she didn't even need.

We were now in Red Lobster's because this of course, was her favorite restaurant and anything baby girl wanted baby girl got.

"Daddy I'm having a great time with you today," She stated taking a sip of her drink.

"I'm having a great time too baby even though I'm practically broke now," I joked with her.

"You're not broke daddy," She giggled.

"And I never will be when it comes to you," I winked at her.

We continued having small talk until the food came and then we both dug in I guess all that shopping we did worked up an appetite.

"This is so good daddy, I just love Red Lobster's," She said placing some food in her mouth.

All I could do was smile, being around her brought out a different side of me, it's like the side of me that the street knew didn't exist when I was with her and I loved that shit.

"Am I still going to meet your new friend daddy?" She asked.

When she asked me that, I took a sip of my drink and had to think about Keri. Right now she wasn't fuckin with me, but that wasn't going to last long so I wasn't even worried about that.

"Soon princess, finish up so I can take you to grandma's house," I responded.

She nodded her head and dug back into her food like I asked her, I continued to stare at her as she ate still in shock that I made that. I couldn't wait to possibly have a little junior running around here, if Keri gets her shit together she could possibly give me that and I would be complete.

"Finished daddy," Kaylee spoke getting my attention.

I grabbed the waitress' attention and signaled for her to bring me the check, so I could pay for it and we can get up out of here. She brought the check over and I pulled out some money that would cover the bill and her tip.

"Let's go princess," I announced.

She got up grabbed my hand and we were out the door and headed to my mom's house. Pulling up to my mom's house, I honked the horn so she could open the door and let Kaylee in.

"I know good and got damn well I taught you better than that to be honking your damn horn," She yelled trying to scold me.

"I'm sorry ma, you did, but I have to go," I told her.

"I don't give a damn."

"I hear you ma, Kaylee go to grandma. I'll see you later baby girl," I told her.

"Okay daddy," She responded getting out her seatbelt.

She leaned to the front kissing me on the cheek before getting out the car closing the door behind her.

"I love you daddy," She stopped and said before turning to run to my mom's arms.

"Love you too, I'll see you soon," I replied winking at her.

"Be careful Cobain," She yelled.

"I will ma, love you too old lady," I joked pulling off.

I pushed my day that I just had with my kid to the back of my mind and got into killer mode. I don't know what Ali did to get Dragon to give Cree back, but the way he moved nothing he did surprised me anymore. So I had to be prepared for anything, I picked up my phone and dialed him up.

"Yo?"

"I'm on my way," I told him.

"Aight bet say less," He replied hanging up the phone.

I turned Future up and made my way to meet my man so we could finally put an end to this beef.

Chapter 12- Cree

I was still sitting in this basement waiting for that crazy nigga to come down here and move this dead body from out of here, shit was really starting to creep me the fuck out. I was still looking around to try and find something I could use to maybe hurt or even kill him with so I could get out of here. As my luck would have it nothing was in this disgusting ass basement. I heard the door open and I ran back to the mattress as if I never left it.

"Put this on and let's go," He yelled tossing me a shirt to put on.

"Where… where are we going?" I asked nervously.

"We're leaving, now hurry up and get dressed," He screamed looking at me with a crazed look in his eyes making me nervous.

I quickly grabbed the shirt and put it on without saying another word. I wasn't sure what changed from when he went upstairs but I wasn't trying to get on his bad side.

"Let's go," He demanded dragging me by my arm up the steps.

When we got upstairs, I looked around to see if I noticed where I was but nothing stood out to me.

"Let's go," He said pulling me out the door.

His henchman opened the back door of a van, but before he put me in, they placed a sheet over my head and tied my hands behind my back. I sat in the back of the van not knowing where I was going next or what had him so spooked all of a sudden. This wasn't the same confident man that I've been seeing all this time.

I was praying the whole ride that I wasn't being taken somewhere to be killed in a field or something. My heart wouldn't stop racing and the unknown was really driving me crazy. All I could do was pray that my life was going to be spared today. I felt the van come to a stop and I just waited to see what was going to happen next. Nobody came and opened the door for the first few minutes, so I was sitting there scared as fuck until I heard a familiar voice.

"I knew you would see things my way," I heard the familiar voice say.

"Ali?" I mumbled to myself.

"Ali and Cobain, I can't say this is a pleasure."

"It wouldn't be for you now would it?" Ali asked.

"Where is my family?"

"They are safe for now, where is Cree?" He asked.

"She's here in the van," I heard him say before I heard the van open making me tense up before I felt myself being pulled out.

"Come on," I heard the man say as we walked a short ways before suddenly stopping.

"Cree, you good?" He called out.

"Ali? Yes please get me out of here," I yelled feeling myself getting emotional from finally hearing him.

"I will baby girl, I'm here now to bring you home. Take that shit off her got damn face. She aint no damn slave" He barked off orders.

They pulled the sheet off my head, and Ali and I immediately locked eyes which prompted me to start crying. I didn't ever think I would see him again.

"You see her. Now where the fuck is my family," He barked.

"Jay bring them out."

I was still standing there, not really understanding what was going on. I just hoped that he was here to finally bring me home.

"What the fuck happened to my wife's shoulder?" He yelled.

"She got shot, what the fuck you think happened. The bitch pulled out on me and almost shot me. Call it a reflex," He spoke in a sarcastic tone.

"Daddyyyyyy," I heard some kids cry out.

"Its okay kids, we are going home soon," He assured the kids I heard crying.

"Man I don't have all day for this fuck shit. Give me my girl so I can go about my business," He stated in a matter of fact tone.

"Walk," Dee said pushing me towards Ali.

I didn't even walk as soon as I got the push, I took off running towards him and didn't stop until I was safely in his arms.

"I got you Cree baby, I'm so sorry. Shhh, don't cry," He whispered in my ears.

"NOW GIVE ME MY FAMILY," He demanded.

"Come on let's go to the car, Jay give him his family," He yelled as he walked me towards an awaiting car.

Cobain stood there and watched as the exchange was made as I was getting in the car. Ali didn't get in with me instead, he closed the door and went back to stand by Cobain.

"Now I take it that we won't have any more problems from you?"

"He didn't speak he just looked at him and nodded his head, even though I could tell that he really didn't want to agree but right now he didn't have any other options.

"Good, it was nice doing business with you and fuck you very much," He spoke while walking away back toward the car along with Cobain.

I watched as he gathered his family and put them in another car that had pulled up; he took one more look at us then winked sending chills down my body before he got in the car.

"What if he comes back for me?" I asked in a whisper.

"He won't, I promise."

"How do you know?" I asked not even looking up to look at him.

"Driver, stop the car," He ordered.

The driver did as he was told and I looked up at Ali to see what he was about to say.

"Look," He told me pointing out the window.

I looked past him and out the window and that's when I saw a guy with a rifle shoot and it hit the gas tank making the whole car explode.

"That's how I know., I know he wouldn't have stopped coming for us especially since I involved his family, so I had to do what I had to do to prevent that. So when I say you have nothing to worry about I mean it," He explained.

I nodded my head and laid back on his shoulder closing my eyes finally thankful that this part of my life was coming to an end.

***

I woke up in a cold sweat in a bedroom that I didn't recognize; I looked around scared that I had gotten kidnapped again.

"Shhh don't be scared I'm here don't worry," Ali spoke trying to sooth me.

"I... thought... he... got... me... again," I said feeling myself about to hyperventilate.

"Breathe Cree, deep breaths," He tried to coach me.

He got up and grabbed me some water to drink. He placed the cup to my lips and I slowly drank.

"Thank you," I smiled weakly at him.

"Listen I know you went through hell, but I will be here with you every step of the way to help you," He told me in the most sincere voice.

I just looked at him and smiled again. My mind was all over the place right now and I wasn't really sure what I wanted from him.

"I see your mind racing, talk to me babe," He urged looking at me.

"I'm scared honestly. Every time I close my eyes I think I'm back in that place and it freaks me out and I can't breathe," I admitted.

"I can't say I know what you're experiencing because I don't, but I'm sorry that you had to go through whatever it is that you had to go through down there. A part of me wants to know what happened, but the other part of me doesn't wanna know. I'm afraid I won't be able to handle whatever you tell me," He stated sounding defeated.

I didn't even respond to him. I put my head down feeling myself getting emotional all over again.

"Cree when you got snatched, I lost it and it took me back to a place that I was trying to never revisit. I don't think you really understand that I was ready to go to war behind this… behind you."

I listened to everything he was saying and that's when it clicked in my head, he was talking about his old girl that got snatched and killed. There was an awkward silence that was between us. I guess we were both in our heads about everything that went on.

"Did they rape you?" He blurted out randomly without looking at me.

"No," I replied.

I finally heard him let go of the breath he was holding when he asked me that question.

"Listen, I just want to apologize to you ma for what happened to you behind my situation. I never meant for any of that to happen you have to believe me."

"I know," I replied.

He picked up my hand and kissed it while still looking at me.

"Ali," I started.

"What's up ma you need something?"

"No, just listen, this, whatever this is isn't going to work for me anymore," I started.

"What the fuck does that mean?" He jumped up.

"Calm down and please listen. I always told myself that after my last relationship, I wouldn't deal with guys like you anymore,"

"Guys like me?" He questioned.

"Yes, like you, in the life. My last relationship ended with my man getting shot while we were heading to the movies and that shit traumatized me. After that, I promised myself I wouldn't date like that again. Getting taken by that man only opened up old wounds for me that I never wanted to ever revisit, being with you will only remind me of the past that I'm so desperately trying to get away from," I explained,

"What are you saying Cree?"

"I don't want to be with you anymore, it's too much for me," I told him truthfully not wanting to lead him on anymore.

"Nah I'm not even trying to hear that right now. Fuck all that shit you talking right now. This right here is far from over," He stated pointing between the both of us.

"Ali, I tried to stay away from you but you just had to be persistent and make me fall for you, but the truth of the matter is that I don't feel safe with you," I admitted looking him in the eye.

"Wow, that's how you really feel?" He asked in a surprised tone of voice.

"Honestly, I'm conflicted with my feelings for you and my fear of something happening to either of us."

"I can protect you Cree," He stated in matter of fact tone.

"Like you did this time, right?" I asked sarcastically.

"That's not fair Cree," He said seriously.

"And neither was me getting kidnapped behind some shit you got yourself into," I threw right back.

"You know what all this arguing we doing right now isn't getting us anywhere. Your clearly still tired, so I'm going to let you get some rest and we will discuss this tomorrow when you are feeling a little better," He told me as he was getting up and walking towards the door.

"Ali, I mean it. This right here is no more," I told him pointing between the both of us.

"Real shit ma, you not getting rid of me that easy. You done fucked around and made me fall for you and now you wanna leave a nigga, nah that's not happening. If you need a few days, cool. I'll give you that but that's ALL you're getting," He stated in a matter of fact tone walking out and closing the door behind him leaving me there alone thinking what the fuck did I just get myself into.

Chapter 13- Keri

I pulled up to my house and shut the car off. I looked around and didn't see Max's car anywhere which I was happy about. I got out the car and walked up to the front door letting myself in. I stood in the foyer and just looked around at my house; this was my dream house and everything I wanted I got. Max told me I had no budget when it came to decorating this house. I was supposed to make beautiful memories here, but instead I had nothing but horrible memories that I never wanted to remember.

I walked around looking at every picture that we had up. We lived a wonderful happy life in the public, but behind closed doors you would never believe what was really going on here. All the makeup I had to buy to cover up the bruises, all the arguments we had, just the constant yelling it got tiring and repetitive after a while.

Walking up the steps and making my way to the bedroom, I couldn't help the chills that went down my body as I looked at all the pictures of Cobain and I that were scattered the floor and instant flashbacks of when he beat me started coming back to me. I willed myself not to cry right now. I picked up the picture and traced the outline of Cobain's face, he was all the man that I wanted but didn't know how to let go of this hurt and pain that I was carrying around and let him love me.

I picked up all the pictures on the floor and put them in the trash and looked around my bedroom. This room was so full negative energy not one happy thought ever. If these walls could talk they would have stories to tell the world. I sat on the bed and tried to think of what my next move was about to be, considering it was about to be my best move.

I picked up my phone and was about to dial Cree and then remembered she was still missing. This was all beginning to be too much right now and I didn't know how much more I could take

I put my phone down next to me on the bed and just looked around my room, not really knowing what to do now.

"Fuck it."

I got up and went to my closet and pulled out my suitcase and opened it up on the bed. I started throwing everything that I could inside of it. Whatever I couldn't bring I would just buy again. I went in my safe and pulled out all my important documents that I was going to need and placed them on the bed next to my phone. I went back in my closet and just threw more of my stuff in my luggage filling it until I couldn't anymore.

I ran in Khloe's room and did the same in there. I threw a bunch of her stuff in her suitcase and whatever I didn't remember I would just buy for her as well, but she wasn't coming home from the hospital to stay here anymore. We both deserved more and that's exactly what I was going to give us, we were out of here. I don't know where we were going just yet but it wasn't going to be here.

Once I felt like I had enough of her stuff I brought it downstairs and placed it by the door then went back upstairs and gathered some more of my stuff and brought it all down placing it by the door. I went upstairs and walked back into my bedroom and just looked around at everything, nothing about this room screamed happy. I went to the hall closet and grabbed the baseball bat that we had in there and walked back in the room and just started swinging. I swung on all our pictures that were on the dressers.

    I swung on the pictures that adorned the walls shattering them instantly. I walked into his side of the closet and dropped the bat then started pulling all his clothes off the hangers and dropping them on the floor. I took out all his expensive watches and cufflinks dropping them on the floor, crushing them all under the bat. I went in the bathroom and grabbed the bleach from under the sink and started bleaching all his suits. Everything that had to do with him I was destroying. I didn't care what it was or how much it cost.

By the time I was done, our once beautiful bedroom looked like a hurricane had come through it. Everything of his that had value I destroyed just like he destroyed my life over the years. I went downstairs and started putting our luggage in the car so I could get ready to leave this life behind.

I walked pass this picture that was on the little table, I stopped and picked it up. This was one of our happy days before the abuse started. I couldn't help the smile that came across my face. I really did love this man and all he did was hurt me as soon as he slid that ring on my finger. I dropped the picture shattering the glass in the frame, then looked at my ring finger which adorned a beautiful 10K princess cut diamond ring. I remember when he first proposed to me with it, I was over the moon ecstatic and couldn't wait to start planning my wedding.

That happiness I felt didn't last long. It's like as soon as I said yes, a switch in his brain turned on and the crazy came out. I shook my head trying to erase those memories as I slowly slid the ring off dropping it to the floor. I ran back upstairs to grab my phone and documents. I took one last look at the room and chucked up my deuces and walked back downstairs and made my way out the door leaving my old life behind me.

I closed the door making sure to lock it behind me then dropping the keys in the mailbox.

"Going somewhere?" I heard from behind me.

Chapter 14- Ali

I couldn't get me and Cree's last conversation out of my head, shit was really fuckin' with my mental. I haven't been feeling a shorty since I lost Ashanti, and now I might have lost her behind this fuck shit. I don't think she realizes that shit fucked with me just as much as it fucked with her. I was sitting in my living room rolling up pissed the fuck off.

I heard footsteps getting closer, but I wasn't worried because only certain people knew the code to my house and since I really didn't fuck with nobody else, I knew it was only one person.

"Yo what it do bro?" Cobain asked walking into the living room.

"Can't call it," I replied before I licked my backwood to seal it.

"Where ol girl at? She still resting?" He questioned as he sat down across from me.

"Man hell nah, I went to go check this morning and her ass had dipped somehow," I told him feeling myself getting pissed off all over again.

"What you mean gone?"

"What you think I mean? Her ass up and disappeared on a nigga in the middle of the night after she told me she didn't wanna fuck with me no more," I explained.

"WORD?" He said shocked covering his mouth.

"Right," I replied shaking my head.

I lit the blunt and took a hard pull so I could try and calm my nerves because the way I was feeling a nigga was ready to go find Cree's ass and bring her back here and not let her ass out until she decided to make shit work with me again.

"So, what are you going to do?"

"Honestly, I don't know. I'm feeling the hell outta shorty and I get that what happened to her was fucked up, but she can't hate a nigga forever for that," I stated truthfully.

"I hear what you saying bro but you have to look at it from her point of view and stop thinking only about yourself. We don't even know what happened to her down there; shorty might be traumatized and shit. She just might need a minute to get her thoughts together," He tried to explain.

"Man fuck all that shit, she can get her thoughts together up in the spare bedroom. I'm fucked up behind this shit too nigga," I barked.

"I feel you bro but you being selfish as fuck right now," He told me in a matter of fact tone.

"I don't give a fuck," I yelled taking another pull of my blunt.

I looked over at him and he was just shaking his head laughing at me but I didn't care. I meant what the fuck I said.

"Pass the fuckin' blunt," He said through laughter.

I took another pull then passed it to him; I shouldn't have given his ass shit since he had the fuckin' giggles all of a sudden.

"How's the doc?" I asked sitting back in my chair.

"I don't know," He replied taking a pull.

"What the fuck you mean you don't know?" I asked sitting up in my chair.

"What I said I don't know bro," He repeated.

He begin telling me how him and her got into it at his place and she stormed out leaving him there and he hasn't seen her since.

"Damn bro, we sure know how to pick em," I joked.

"Tell me about it," He chuckled passing me back the blunt.

We both sat there in the living room passing the blunt back and forth not saying a word to each other, but saying a lot.

"I have to kill this nigga Max," Cobain blurted out randomly.

"Who in the fuck is Max and why do we have to kill him?" I questioned.

"We?" He chuckled.

"Yeah nigga you heard me, WE now, what the fuck he do to us?" I asked.

"That's Keri's fiancé; ol boy gotta go," He stated.

"You know how you wanna handle it?" I inquired looking at him seriously.

"I'm trying to put some shit together, when it's all finalized, I'll let you know."

"Say less," I replied.

We both sat there lost in our thoughts. After the blunt was finished, I was thinking how I was going to get my girl back before I lost her ass for good.

Chapter 15- Cree

Soon as that nigga left out the room, I already had it in my mind that I was leaving out of his shit. That nigga clearly had me fucked up. Fuck all that hot shit he was talking. I wasn't even trying to hear it, I had my mind made up and I meant everything that I said. I wasn't fuckin with him anymore. Soon as I thought the coast was clear, I ordered me an Uber and took my ass the fuck home.

I was now in the safety of my own home soaking my body in a hot tub full of Epsom salt; this was feeling like everything right now. As much as I liked Ali he came with too much drama and I didn't need that in my life right now. I soaked in the tub for about two hours letting the water out and refilling it until I didn't want to be in here anymore. After about another thirty more minutes, I finally decided to get out the tub.

I grabbed my towel and wrapped it around my body and stood and looked at my reflection in the mirror. I looked at the bruise that was under my eye and slowly brought my hand up to it and touched it and instantly got pissed all over again. I reached in my cabinet and pulled out the cocoa butter and put some on the bruise so it wouldn't leave a mark.

I walked out the bathroom and sat on my bed and just cried in my hands. I was so emotional and it was really bothering me because I wasn't this person. I can't believe that I really went through what I just went through. Never in my life would I ever think that I would have been there. I finally got myself a little together and decided a nap was something that I needed, after that I needed to go get me a new phone.

I dropped my towel and got into my bed naked and sleep immediately came to me.

"Jameer, baby can we please go to the movies later?" I begged my boyfriend.

"Not today babe, I got some runs to make and shit is a little hot right now," He explained.

"Whatever, everything and everyone is always more important than me," I fake pouted.

"Nah not even baby, you know nobody is more important than you," He stated placing a kiss on my lips.

"Your actions are showing me different," I said before sticking my tongue out at him.

"Uggggg you make shit so complicated, fuck it you wanna go to the movies, we will go to the movies. Whatever Cree wants Cree gets. You happy now, you big ass baby?"

"I am now, thank you baby," I smiled hugging him tight.

"I bet man get off me," He joked pushing me away.

"Stop," I whined.

"Pick a show time," He said walking into the closet.

"I already did," I told him covering my face.

"Oh, you just knew that I was going to change my mind huh?" He said peeking his head out the closet.

"Nooooo… yes," I laughed.

"You make me sick," He laughed shaking his head.

"I love you too baby," I responded,

I waited for him to finish getting dressed so we could go to the movies and then he could go do whatever the hell he needed to do. Jameer and I have been together since I could remember. When we first met, he told me I was going to be his girl one day and of course I didn't believe him and brushed it off. Fast forward years later, and now we were inseparable. You never saw one without the other unless he was handling business and even than I wasn't too far behind. I always had my nigga's back. I was with him from the beginning as he started to slowly build his empire from the ground up and start to make a name for himself around town. He was my first and hopefully my last and the love of my life.

"Babe come on the movie starts in forty-five minutes," I yelled.

"I'm coming woman," He responded walking out the closet pulling his shirt down.

"Don't you look good, let me find out you trying to impress somebody," I joked.

"Man shut your ass up, how about you impress this dick later on when we get back," He told me grabbing his crotch making me roll my eyes.

"If you get me a large popcorn and two boxes of sour patch watermelon, I'll do whatever you like," I spoke seductively.

"Let's go you want nachos too baby?" He joked pulling me towards the door.

"You're such an asshole," I laughed as he continued to pull me to the car.

"I'm your asshole though," He winked opening the passenger door for me.

I slid inside as he closed the door behind me and jogged around the driver side and got in.

"So, where we going?" He asked starting the car.

"Fresh Meadows," I told him.

"Bet."

He pulled out in route to the movies; we cracked jokes on each other the entire way there as we always did when we were together. We were just two big goofballs around each other and I wouldn't change our relationship for the world.

"You know you gonna be my wife one day soon, right?" He randomly said looking over at me catching me off guard.

"Well is that so?" I asked with the raise of my eyebrow.

"Hell the fuck yeah, I'm in this for keeps and besides I broke that pussy in and I'll be damned if I let another mother fucker get up in there," He stated in a matter of fact tone.

"You can never just be serious," I told him rolling my eyes.

"Nah baby girl that's where you got it messed up, I'm 100 percent serious," He told me as he picked up my hand and kissed the back of it making me blush.

"Well you already know if you rockin' I'm rolling."

"That's what I like to hear," He smiled.

We continued to drive to the theatre making small talk, but something wasn't sitting right with me. I started looking around and noticed that we were being followed.

"Babe make this left real quick," I told him.

He did it without even asking why I told him to.

"I knew it," I mumbled.

"Knew what?" He questioned.

"Were being followed," I told him.

"Aight bet, pass me my gun babe," He told me as calm as he could.

I looked at my side mirror and saw that the car was still trailing us, as I reached under my seat and pulled out his gun out and handed it over to him. We stopped at a red light and the car pulled up alongside of us. I tried to get a look at whoever it was but the tints were too dark for me to see anything.

"Babe hold on," He told me as he floored it through the red light.

Soon as he pulled off the car wasn't too far behind us, Jameer was dipping and dodging through traffic trying to get away.

"Ahhh," I yelled as the back window was shot out.

"Shit, babe keep your head down," He yelled trying to get away from the car.

He made a quick right and tried to lose them but it didn't work they were still on our ass. Jameer managed to get a few shots off as he kept trying to lose them.

"Stay down Cree," He yelled.

I did as he told me and kept my eyes closed as all the windows started shattering all around me.

"Shit babe, drive this car," I shouted.

He did a sharp turn and pulled into an alley and shut the car off.

"Why you stop babe?" I asked in a panic tone.

"I think I lost them, let's try and make a run for it,"

"What? Hell no, I'm not getting out this car and you need to start this car and drive the hell away from here," I yelled.

"Cree baby, we can't they know my car. Their looking for it, we have to try and make it on foot," He explained.

"I don't want to," I told him feeling myself getting emotional.

"Cree trust me I got you," He told me looking me in the eyes.

"Okay," I replied looking at him. I trusted this man with my life and I know he wouldn't let anything happen to me.

He leaned over and kissed me before we both got out the car and tried to make a run for it. We held hands and ran to the end of the alley which I wish we hadn't done because we walked right into the end of a gun.

"Jameer my nigga," His friend Liam said with a grin on his face.

"Liam what the fuck nigga? This is what we doing right now?" Jameer screamed.

"It's nothing personal, you still my nigga. It's just business," He told him before shooting him in the head.

"AHHHHHHHHHHHH"

"Shut the fuck up, now what did you see?" He asked pointing the gun at me.

"No... Nothing" I stuttered as the tears fell down my face as I looked down at Jameer's lifeless body bleeding out.

"Good," He stated turning around and jogging back to his car leaving me standing there.

"Jameer" I cried.

I couldn't be seen with him here like this I didn't need the cops questioning me about anything. I took one last look at him and kissed my hand and then placed it on his cheek.

"I love you," I whispered.

I ran back to his car and grabbed the gun and the rest of my belongings then left him there.

DING DONG… DING DONG…

My doorbell ringing woke me up from that horrible nightmare that I was just having.

"Fuck," I mumbled.

I looked down at my body and I was covered in sweat. I hated thinking about Jameer, he was always a sore spot for me. I always tried to keep him and his memories in the back of my mind.

DING DONG

"I'm coming" I yelled.

I wrapped my towel back around my body and went to open the door, I couldn't wait to get back in the shower, I was feeling so nasty and sticky. I made it downstairs and looked through my peephole and instantly got annoyed with who was there.

I opened the door and just stared at them.

"What the hell are you doing here?" I asked folding my arms across my chest.

"It's nice to see you too," Ali said walking into my house right past me.

"Excuse me," I turned and looked at him.

"Close the door and come sit down we about to talk and figure this shit the fuck out. We aren't leaving this bitch until we come to a mutual agreement," He stated sitting in the living room.

I just rolled my eyes and slammed the door. I wasn't beat for his shit and wasn't about to deal with it right now. I walked right past him and went straight to my bedroom and slammed the door.

"You can slam the door all you want I'll be right here when you come back down," He yelled.

"Asshole."

Chapter 16- Cobain

Two days later…

I had a plan already in motion for Max's bitch ass. I was waiting for my guy to come through with what I needed. So, while I was waiting for him, I had to go to the hospital and bring Shyne's ass home. I just knew she was about to be a pain in my ass, but if she knew what was good for her she wouldn't piss me off.

I pulled up to the hospital and walked straight to her room. Soon as I walked in I saw the doctor was there talking to her and giving her discharge papers.

"My fault for my lateness doc, what were you explaining to her?" I asked shaking the doctor's hand,

"Well I was just telling her about her at home care for her scar and for her to take it easy, and she's not allowed to lift anything over ten pounds," He explained.

"Bet, I'll make sure she follows your orders, does she have any meds or anything?" I asked him because I couldn't trust her ass.

"Yes, I gave her all the prescriptions and information that she will need when she gets home," He explained.

"Aight cool, thank you for everything," I responded shaking his hand.

"No problem, a nurse will be in shortly with a wheelchair to escort you guys out," He explained before walking out.

"Thanks for coming Cobain," She spoke sincerely.

"Who the hell else was going to come for you Shyne?" I asked already getting annoyed.

"I'm just saying thank you damn, why you have to always be so damn defensive,"

"Man, we wouldn't even be here right now, if you didn't go all *"Thin line between love and hate"* and shoot your damn self," I told her straight up.

"Well if you would just give me what I asked for then I wouldn't have had to go to those extremes," She sassed.

"Shyne, why can't you ever get it through your head that there will never be an us. You will forever be the mother of my child nothing more, nothing less," I tried to explain for the millionth time.

She sucked her teeth and rolled her eyes mad at my answer but I didn't care that's what the fuck it was going to be, and the sooner she gets that out of her head the better off she would be. I was getting real tired of repeating myself to a grown ass woman.

"I heard someone is going home today," This happy ass nurse came in with a big ass smile on her face.

"Yeah girl I'm finally out of here," Shyne replied to her fake pouting.

She helped her into the wheelchair as I gathered her belongings for us to leave; we walked out the room and headed towards the elevator. I ignored all their little girl talk that they were having, and all the childish ass laughing. I couldn't wait to drop her off and go about my business.

We got downstairs and I left them in the lobby while I went and pulled the car around to the entrance. When I came back around I saw her handing the nurse back her phone. I assumed she put her number in there. I hope that nurse will help her want to get her life together and make her want to get a job.

I got out the car and walked around to open the passenger side door to open it up as she wheeled her outside. I grabbed her hand and helped her inside the car as gentle as I could, since I saw her wincing in pain when she stood. I closed the door behind her and walked back to my side and got in and pulled right off.

"So I was thinking."

Here she goes with the fuck shit already, I was just trying to drop her off and go not have a therapy session.

"What were you thinking Shyne?" I asked turning to look at her quickly.

"I was thinking that I could stay with you until I'm completely healed," She suggested.

"Hell nah,"

"Damn tell me how you really feel," She replied with attitude.

"I'm sorry, that came out wrong but nah you can't stay with me Shyne," I told her.

"Why not Cobain? I will need help for a little while and I can't take care of Kaylee like I need to while I'm like this," She added.

"Shit man," I mumbled to myself.

I thought about it for a few and she was right for the most part and I didn't want to keep Kaylee at my mom's house when I had to make moves because I never know how long I'd be out. Against my better judgment, I reluctantly agreed to have her stay with me while she heals completely.

"Fine, you can stay in the spare bedroom, I'll get Kaylee from my mom house then I will drop you both off back at my house," I explained.

"Okay, thank you," She smiled.

"As soon as your ass is better you going home, and don't get any ideas because you aint staying," I warned.

"Okay,"

I drove the rest of the way hoping and praying that I wasn't making a mistake letting her stay with me.

***

I had Shyne set up in the spare bedroom; I had gotten her a nurse to look after her while she was here. She was starting in the morning; Kaylee was in her room watching television as usual. Shit felt weird with all of us being under the same roof. Yeah I use to stay at her house here and there, but she never stayed at my house.

I looked in on her and she was sleeping peacefully thank God. I quietly closed her door and kept walking until I got to Kaylee's room, I peeked in on her and saw her that she was under her covers holding on to her teddy that she's had since she was a baby watching television. Once I saw that she was good I slowly tried to close the door.

"So, you really wasn't going to say goodnight daddy?" She asked never removing her eyes from the TV.

"How you know I was in here?" I asked as I chuckled walking into her room.

"I always know when your close to me your my daddy." She stated with a smile on her face showing off her missing tooth.

"Is that so?" I questioned sitting on the bed.

"Yup," She replied getting up and sitting on my lap.

I couldn't picture my life without Kaylee in it now that's she's here; she makes me want to be a better me.

"You know I love you right baby girl?" I asked pulling her away making her look me in the eyes.

"Yes, daddy and I love you too," She responded as she laid back down on my chest.

I just sat there and held her, I loved that she was here with me for these last few days. It made coming home at night a lot better.

"Are me and mommy staying here forever daddy?" She asked.

"No baby girl, I'm just helping mommy out for a little while, but you know you can stay here with as long as you want," I told her.

"I know, but I don't want to leave mommy alone. She will miss me and I don't want to make her sad," She explained.

"You are so smart for your age did anyone ever tell you that?"

"Yes, nana did the other day," She laughed.

"Well believe it toots," I joked tickling her.

"STOPPPPPPP," She cried out in laughter.

This is how I always pictured me ending my nights after working hard all day, coming home chopping it up with my princess then taking it down with my lady.

"Okay baby girl, let get you ready for bed."

"Aww I don't wanna," She whined.

"You don't have to go to sleep; you can watch your movie,"

"Okay, thank you," She smiled getting under her covers.

I fixed the covers on her and bent down and kissed her forehead.

"Goodnight Kaylee."

"Goodnight daddy," She smiled.

I took one lasts look at her and walked towards the door, and just smiled at my creation.

"Daddy wait we didn't sing our song," She called out before I was able to close the door.

"That's right we didn't," I replied walking back in the room and sitting on the bed next to her.

"Ready?" She asked.

"Always," I replied.

She grabbed my hand and smiled as we started singing our song.

"No one loves me like you do, no one knows me like you do,

No one can compare, to the way my eyes fit in yours,

You'll always be my father, and I'll always be your joy,

I tried to match your breathing, beating my little heart against yours,

Perfect were the nights, we were sleepin' I never wanna end what we are"

"Goodnight baby girl," I said again giving her one last kiss.

"Night daddy," She replied turning over in the bed.

I got up and walked out the room quietly closing the door behind me. I went downstairs and wasn't even shocked to see this nigga Ali on my couch with the bottle and two shot glasses waiting.

"This nigga always coming through with the clutch," I laughed walking into the living room giving him dap then sitting down.

"You already know," He laughed.

He popped open the bottle pouring us both a shot, we held it up then took it straight back.

"Shit smooth."

"Hell yeah," He replied pouring us both another shot.

"So, check it, Shyne is upstairs," I admitted.

"Wait… run that by me again," He said with a confused face.

"It's nothing to run by you nigga, I just told you Kylee and Shyne are upstairs," I stated taking my shot back.

"I get why baby girl is upstairs, but why is her crazy ass unstable ass mama up there?" He questioned.

"She wasn't comfortable home alone with Kaylee while she was still healing, so I let her stay in the spare bedroom until she's better then she's outta here." I explained.

"I hear you, I just hope this shit doesn't backfire on you," He said laughing.

"What the fuck are you talking about?"

"You know Shyne isn't wrapped to tight, something is going to happen, mark my words," He told me.

"Nah not this time, I really think she got it through her head," I said not really believing the words I was saying.

"For your sake I hope it's true."

We sat there going over shit and tossing back shots until the wee hours of the night until he finally decided that he was ready to go. When he left I locked up behind him and went straight upstairs to my room and closed my door and just fell across my bed and knocked out from all the alcohol I consumed.

Chapter 17- Keri

"What are you doing here?" I asked my mom as I walked down the steps.

"I came to see how you were doing, Max told me what happened between you guys," She admitted.

"I bet he did. So why are you here? To tell me not to leave him, oh wait Keri what did you do for him to hit you? I told you to stay out of his way," I replied mocking her.

"That's not how I sound."

"What do you want mother, I have to go," I stated in an aggravated tone of voice.

"Go? Where are you going Keri?" She questioned.

"The hell away from here, I can't and won't do this with him anymore, and there's nothing you can say that will change my mind," I told her.

"Keri just wait hear me out, please?" She asked.

"What ma," I asked as I blew out a breath of frustration.

"I know I haven't always been the best mom to you or your sister growing up but I tried my best," She explained.

"Your best huh? Was your best drinking until you pass out leaving me to cook and look after Khloe? Was your best when you had multiple men coming and going. I have called so many different men uncles I don't even know who was really family! Was your best getting so high that you almost overdosed and I had to get Cree to help me get you in a cold shower to try and wake you back up?"

"OKAY KERI DAMN I GET IT, I WASN'T THE BEST MOM," She yelled.

"That's an understatement."

"Listen I didn't come here for that, that's the past and we are going to leave it there. I came to see if you were okay," She told me.

I knew my mother better then she thinks I do, and that's not the reason why she came over here. She always wants to be a victim and a bully and that's just not how life worked. I can almost guarantee that she came over to pick my brain about Max.

"Where are you going?" She asked looking around.

"I'm going to get me and Khloe a new place. We can't stay here anymore, you do remember your other daughter, right? The one you have yet to ask about" I looked at her titling my head to the side.

"Of course, I remember her, where is she?"

"She in the hospital mom, but then again you'd know that if you weren't so busy trying to get me to stay with an abuser," I stated in a matter of fact tone.

"IN THE HOSPITAL, FOR WHAT? OH MY GOD! WHY DIDN'T YOU TELL ME?" She yelled being all dramatic making me roll my eyes.

"Max," was all I said.

"What did he do?" She questioned.

I stood there and explained to her what he had told me the day when he beat me, the look of shock on her face told me that she didn't know what happened which I was glad about because if she knew and didn't say anything I was liable to strangle her right here.

"I can't believe he did that shit to my baby girl, is she okay?"

"She's getting better, I'll be picking her up soon," I told her.

"Okay good, I can't believe he pulled that fuck shit on my daughter he could have killed her," She said sounding pissed off.

"He could have killed me plenty of times and that didn't seem to bother you much."

"KERI," She called.

"It's cool ma, I don't really expect different from you. You always treated us differently," I told her truthfully.

"That's not true Keri," She exclaimed.

"Okay ma, if you say so," I replied rolling my eyes at her about to get in my car.

"Wait, can we get something to eat together?" She asked.

I really didn't want to be bothered with her anymore then I already was, she knew how to bring me out of character and I wasn't even trying to take it there with her today.

"Please," She begged.

"Fine," I replied against my better judgment.

She walked around and got in the passenger side of the car and I got in the driver side and pulled off to the local diner. I cut the radio on and made the drive, I didn't want to talk about shit with her. I kept my eyes on the road the whole time until she cut down my radio.

"Keri,"

I took a deep breath and counted to ten in my head before I even responded to her.

"Yes ma," I replied never taking my eyes off the road.

"I know Max has done some fucked up shit to the both of you but I still don't believe he really meant it. I'm sure if you talk to him, y'all can come to some sort of agreement and get back together. "You know he-Was all she was able to get out before I pulled the car over.

"Get out."

"What?" She asked looking around confused.

"Get out," I repeated.

"I'm not getting out; we are in the middle of nowhere. And I am your mother," She stated like that really mattered to me.

"You don't act like it, you would think Max was your son the way you go to bat for him, and I don't have the time to deal with your shit today. Now get out," I stated looking at her seriously.

"Keri, we are in the middle of nowhere, and you just expect to get out?"

"Yeah well you should have thought about that before you started running your mouth, now as I said GET OUT," I shrugged.

She took off her seatbelt and slowly got out my car making sure to slam the door behind her. I rolled the window down and said one last thing before I pulled off leaving her to think about her actions.

"Just to show you I'm not in complete bitch mode I'll order you an Uber and send it your way," I told her as I pulled off.

"KERI… KERI…" She continued to yell behind the car.

I politely rolled my window down and stuck my hand out waving at her leaving her behind.

Chapter 18- Ali

I sat on Cree's couch waiting for her to come back downstairs, I don't know what the fuck she thought I was dead ass serious when I told her I wasn't letting her go. Since I was still high, I walked into her kitchen opening her fridge pulling out some lunch meat and some mayo, along with some lettuce and tomato, then looked around for the bread. Once I had what I needed I made myself a sandwich fit for a king. I then grabbed a beer out and went back to the living room and waited for her to come join me.

I kicked off my sneakers and grabbed the remote control turning it on; I turned to Starz since I missed the last episode of Power. Once I got it started, I tossed the remote and bit into my sandwich. I picked up this girly ass beer and popped the top and took a swig of it, putting it back down to finish my sandwich.

"What the fuck is a Blue Moon?" I mumbled to myself looking at the beer bottle.

I finished off my sandwich and Power was just about over and Cree still hasn't brought her chocolate ass back downstairs yet. When I saw the show was over I took my ass upstairs to find out what the fuck was holding her up when I told her silly ass we had to talk. I got to the top of her stairs and her bedroom door was still closed.

"This woman is just as hardheaded as she wants to be."

I went to open the door and the shit was locked.

"Aint this bout a bitch," I mumbled.

I started banging on the door as loud as I could.

"Cree open the got damn door," I yelled banging on the door.

"GO AWAY ALI," She responded.

"Hell nah, you knew I was downstairs waiting on your scary ass and you up here locked in the damn room. Why the fuck you being so damn rude like your mama didn't raise you better Cree?"

"Shut the fuck up, I told you I didn't wanna talk to you. I don't know why you still here its been over an hour," She shouted from behind the door.

"Cree, I will shoot this fuckin' door down if you don't open it," I yelled.

"I told you I needed time; if you leave and give me time I promise I will call you,"

"Man, hell nah we about to talk about this shit NOW, fuck you think this is? I'm not leaving here until we talk," I stated.

"BYE ALI."

"Bet," I replied.

I don't know why she thought I was playing with her ass, I meant what the fuck I said when I said we were going to talk today and figure out this situation. I walked out her house and went in my car and grabbed my gun putting the silencer on it and walking back into her house slamming the door behind me.

I walked back up the stairs and knocked on the door with the handle of the gun.

"Cree are you going to open the door?"

"NO THE FUCK I'M- "

POP... POP... BOOM.

"AHHHHH," She screamed jumping up off the bed.

"I told your simple ass to open the damn door now look what you made me do," I told her walking into her room.

"WHY THE FUCK WOULD YOU SHOOT MY FUCKIN' DOOR DOWN FOR?" She yelled as she picked up a picture frame and threw it at me.

"Watch that shit Cree," I threatened.

"So… get…the…fuck…out!" She screamed as she threw different stuff at me after each word.

I looked at her and pointed the gun at her making her freeze up and look at me like I was crazy.

"Sooooo, you gonna shoot me Ali?" She asked with a tilt of her head.

"I don't want to but I'll shoot you in your big toe if you don't stop throwing shit at me." I told her straight up as lowered my gun.

"What do you want? She asked in a defeated tone of voice.

"I just want to talk,"

"Fine, let's go downstairs and talk," She said with attitude.

"Thank you, that's all I've been asking for the last hour."

"Shut up Ali, and you getting my damn door fixed," She stated.

"Bet, ONLY if I like what I hear after we talk," I stated.

I walked out the room and followed her back down the stairs to her living room where we both sat across from each other and just stared at one another.

"So, what was so important that you had to shoot down my door and obviously make yourself at home down here?" She asked me like she didn't already know the answers to that.

"Why the fuck did you sneak out like a thief in the night Cree?" I asked getting right to the point.

"I had to go; you weren't trying to understand what I was saying to you,"

"Real shit, I still don't understand the shit you was talking earlier," I told her shrugging my shoulders.

"What don't you understand Ali? I can't fuck with you like that anymore," She stated looking me seriously.

"Why?"

"It's just too much honestly," She told me.

"What is?" I asked curiously.

"Nothing, forget it," She said getting up and walking out the living room.

I got up and followed her as she walked into the kitchen and watched as she opened a bottle of water and drank it all.

"Cree," I called out.

"Fine damn man."

We both walked back into the living room and had a seat, I sat across from her and waited for her to talk She began telling me about her past, basically how she fell in love with a dope boy that got killed in front of her and ever since then she swore them off. She said after him she couldn't see herself back in another situation like that, so when that shit with Dragon popped off it brought up all those memories that she tried to keep hidden. By the time she was done with her story her face was wet from the tears.

"Damn Cree," I finally replied shaking my head.

I looked around and saw she had a tissue box on one of her tables, so I reached over and got one then walked and sat next to her handing her the tissue then pulled her close to me where she rested her head on my shoulder as she wiped her eyes.

"That's some deep shit, and I feel where you coming from but that shit aint happening to me. The shit that happened with Dragon was a misfortune and you just happened to be at the right place but at the wrong time. And because I'm a man about my shit, I apologize that you got caught up in some shit behind me," I told her seriously.

"I appreciate your apology Ali I really do but it still doesn't change the fact that I'm not comfortable dealing with you," She said standing up.

I stood up and grabbed her wrist before she got too far away making her face me.

"Baby girl,"

It was crazy that I didn't even know what to say to her, this was the first time that I was actually speechless when it came to a female.

"Yes Ali?" She responded waiting for me to answer.

I didn't know what to say so I did what I thought I should do in this moment and that was kiss her so that's what I did. I pulled her into me and kissed her like it was my last time seeing her. She moaned in my mouth making my dick jump and immediately getting hard, I palmed her ass before I squeezed it deepening my kiss. I slowly slid the shorts she was wearing down dropping them around her ankles as I backed her onto the couch.

I sat her down and she looked up at me with this look that I couldn't even describe. I got down on my knees and spread her legs up; she had the prettiest pussy that I have ever seen. I licked my lips then smirked at her and dove face first into her pussy making her arch her back and close her legs on my head.

"Come on Cree damn."

"Sorry, I wasn't expecting that," She laughed opening her legs for me.

I shook my head and went right back into what I was doing, I held her legs apart while I went to work on her clit. I bit, sucked, licked and massaged her pussy until I felt her legs shaking.

"Shit, Ali," She panted.

"Cum for me baby," I told her as went back and ate it more.

"I'm about to cummmmmmmm," She yelled before cumin in my mouth.

I looked up at her and wiped mouth with the back of my hand.while She laid there looking like she had just bust the biggest nut in history. I stood up and dropped my pants and kneeled back down and pulled her to the edge of the couch slowly sliding her on my dick.

"SHIIIITTTTTTTTT" I gasped as she got further on my dick.

I took a minute to gather my thoughts as she slowly started to whine on my dick.

"Fuck Cree, that shit feels so good," I told her.

I grabbed her by the waist and started fuckin' her and she was fuckin' me back. She was definitely about that life and a nigga wasn't complaining.

"Nah turn that ass around," I told her pulling out and flipping her over on her stomach sliding right back in her.

"Sssssss Ahhhhhh," She screamed as I entered her from the back.

She started throwing that ass back on my dick as I had a grip on her waist; I looked down as all her juices coated my dick. This shit was so fuckin' good, I slapped her ass as she continued to throw it back on my dick, making my shit jump inside of her.

"ALIIIIII," She yelled as I felt her cum on my dick again.

I continued to assault her pussy as she screamed my name. I was trying to leave my trademark on her shit to make sure she never fucks another nigga again. I felt myself about to cum but I was still trying to hold off longer and I was doing good until she looked back at me and winked making me explode all up in her pussy.

"SHITTTTT, FUCKKKKK, Cree," I moaned squeezing her waist as every drip of sperm left my dick.

Once I was finally done releasing in her, I slapped her ass and watched as it moved like jelly. I slowly slid out of her and pulled my pants up and sat down on the couch, Cree was still sitting there with her ass in the air.

"That was some good shit huh Cree, got your ass stuck… literally," I laughed.

She looked at me and gave me the finger before slowly getting herself together. She picked up her shorts and I couldn't help but to stare at her pretty pussy.

"Just because you probably gave me the best dick I've had in a long time doesn't change the fact that I'm still not fuckin' with you no more," She stated in a matter of fact tone.

"Get the fuck outta here; I'm definitely not going anywhere now that I got the pussy. You got me fucked up," I told her straight up.

"I meant when I said that I was done, lock up on your way out please," She told me as she walked away back up the stairs to her room.

Aint this bout a bitch, I just gave this girl the best dick of her life and she still dubbed me. I'll be dammed.

"AND DON'T FORGET TO SEND SOMEONE TO FIX MY GOT DAMN DOOR," She shouted from upstairs.

"HELL NO, GET YOUR OWN DAMN DOOR FIXED," I yelled back walking out her house slamming the door behind me.

Chapter 19- Shyne

I was feeling better as the days passed so I was up and able to move around better on my own, but not too much as to where Cobain would make me leave. I was enjoying having my little family under the same roof even if it was temporary. I decided that I was going to cook dinner tonight, so I sent the nurse to the store to pick up everything that I was going to need for tonight. Kaylee and I were going to have mommy daughter time getting things in order for daddy when he comes home.

"Kaylee," I called out.

"Yes, mommy," She replied sticking her head in the door.

"You want to help mommy make dinner?" I asked.

"Yes," She replied excitedly.

"Perfect, because mommy is going to need all the help she can get since I'm still in a little pain."

"Okay I'll help you with whatever you need," She smiled.

"That's my pretty princess, we are going to surprise daddy when he comes home," I told her.

"He's going to love that," She replied jumping up and down.

"I know, that's the plan. The nurse already went and picked up everything that we need for dinner so you ready to get started?" I asked.

"Yup."

"Great, let's go," I replied standing up.

We both walked hand and hand downstairs to the kitchen so we could prep for tonight's surprise dinner. When we got in the kitchen the nurse had everything already out on the table waiting for me.

"What are we going to make?"

"We are making cubed steak, mash potatoes, and asparagus and a cake for dessert," I told her.

"A cake? Can I lick the bowl after were done?" She asked as her eyes lit up.

"You sure can," I replied making her show me that toothless smile of hers.

I turned on the stereo and we started dancing and singing along to the song as we got everything together. We were both cutting up peppers and onions and just having a good time together. This is how it should be all the time us preparing dinner for Cobain to come home to, if I have anything to say about it by the time I'm healed up he will be asking me to move in with him. I can just feel it.

About an hour later we had everything on the stove simmering and the cake was about to come out the oven and once that was cooled enough Kaylee would be putting the frosting on it. Kaylee set the table and had everything looking so beautiful; I really couldn't wait until he came home. I knew he would be pissed but he wouldn't say it in front of Kaylee which I was thankful for.

"Mommy I smell the cake," Kaylee announced coming into the living room.

"I bet you do," I laughed getting up off the couch and following her into the kitchen.

I went into the kitchen and grabbed the mitts and opened the oven pulling the cake out placing it on top of the stove.

"It looks soooo pretty mommy,"

"Doesn't it, now go get cleaned up so you can look pretty when daddy come and then we can eat," I suggested.

"Then can I put the icing on the cake?" She pouted.

"Yes, you little spoiled brat," I laughed.

"Okay, thank you mommy," She kissed me then ran to her room to get ready.

While she was getting herself ready I was about to go do the same. I was starting to feel a little pain so when I got to my room I popped a pill then got myself ready for daddy to come home.

***

"What is all of this?" Cobain asked walking into the house.

"We made you dinner and cake daddy," Kaylee responded walking up to him and hugging him.

He bent down and picked her up kissing her on the cheek and looking directly at me.

"You did? Did you?" He replied never taking his eyes off me.

"Yes, mommy and I worked really hard, do you like it daddy?" She questioned.

"I love it baby, now go wash your hands so we can eat," He told her kissing her on the cheek before he put her down.

"Okay," She said then ran out the room.

Once she was out the room his whole mood changed and only if you know the kind of person he was that you would notice it. His eyes went dark when he looked at me.

"What the fuck is going on here Shyne?" He asked in a harsh whisper.

"Nothing she wanted to make you dinner, this was all her idea I just assisted her," I lied.

"Uh huh, I know you Shyne this has you written all over it, but because my baby girl looks so happy about it, I won't fuck you up. But don't tempt me," He told me as he backed me into the corner.

"I'm back daddy," Kaylee announced as she came back in the room.

"I see," He turned and spoke to her looking like he never even just threatened my life.

"You ready to eat?"

"I sure am princess," He replied grabbing her hand as they walked over to the table.

It was so cute to see them together; he pulled her chair out for her allowing her to sit down. He treated her how I wish he treated me, he was showing her the way any man she gets in the future is supposed to treat her and if he didn't then she couldn't fuck with him.

"Come on and sit down mommy," Kaylee said pulling me from my thoughts.

"Here I come baby,"

I sat next to Kaylee and grabbed the both of us plates and started putting food on her plate and handing it to her.

"Thank you, mommy, are you going to make daddy a plate also?" She asked looking at me.

"Ye- "I started to say.

"No princess daddy is going to make his own plate," Cobain told her.

I made my plate and waited until Cobain made his before we all stared to dig in. For the most part dinner was rather quiet besides the millions of questions Kaylee had for both of us. It felt like for a moment we were a normal family and I was enjoying every moment of it, hoping that one day this would be a permanent thing.

"Daddy do you like the food? I helped mommy cut up everything and she let me put the steak in the pot also," She bragged.

"I do it's delicious, you did a good job today," He acknowledged.

She looked up at him and just smiled. The love she had for her father was simply amazing. In her eyes, he was her hero and couldn't do anything wrong. If I didn't do anything right in my life picking Cobain to father my child was the best decision ever.

"Daddy do you want cake?" Kaylee asked looking at him.

"No, but I bet you do," He laughed.

"How did you know?" She giggled.

"I know my baby that's why," He told her.

"Mommy I ate all my food; can I please get a piece of cake now?" She begged.

"Yes, you can," I replied.

"Yaaaay."

I cut her a piece of cake and handed it to her as I started to clear the table off and clean the kitchen. I put the extra food in the fridge and put the dishes in the dishwasher, I was not about to be sitting up here all-night washing dishes. Cobain walked in the kitchen with a bottle in his had then went to the cabinet and grabbed a glass.

I watched as he poured some in the glass and take a drink, he didn't even say one thing to me. I was really starting to get tired of the lack of acknowledgement from him, once I had the kitchen back to its original state; I was going to call it a night. I tried and he didn't even say anything about it. I wiped down the counter one last time and put the rag on the counter and was about to go to my room.

"Shyne," Cobain called.

"Yes," I replied.

"Thank you, dinner was good," He told me.

"You're welcome," I smiled and walked away back to my room, maybe I still had a chance after all.

Chapter 20- Keri

I was heading up to the hospital to finally bring Khloe home. We were going to be staying at Cree's for now until I found us a new place that would work for us. I just knew that we weren't going back home where Max was living. That part of our lives was done and we were not revisiting it ever.

Pulling up to the hospital kind of put me in my feelings, I can't remember a time where I wasn't working and now with so much going on I had to take a leave of absence. I got out the car and grabbed the bag I brought with me filled with clothes and stuff for Khloe to freshen up with before we left the hospital.

I walked into the hospital and stopped by the nurses' station before I made it to Khloe's room.

"How's it going ladies?" I asked walking up on them.

"Oh my God girl we miss you here so much. Dr. Ridgewood is a complete dick and we just miss you please come back," She begged.

"I'll be back soon as I get my life in order," I told her laughing because they were all really back there pouting.

"Y'all saying y'all want me to comeback but as soon as I do y'all going to be talking shit about how hard I am," I joked rolling my eyes.

"No we won't, we've seen the other side and we want no parts of it," They told me making me bust out laughing.

"Shut up, I can't take y'all right now," I said holding my stomach from laughing so much.

"I'm just saying I'll take you any day," She said in a matter of fact tone.

"Whatever let me go check on my sister and get her together, can someone get her discharge papers ready please?" I asked.

"Will do," She replied.

"Thanks," I responded walking away to the room.

Before I walked in the room I got a text from an unknown number that caught me off guard.

Unknown: you not ready to come home yet? C

I already knew who that C belonged to and I still wasn't ready to talk to him yet, so I wasn't. I put the phone in my pocket and walked in my sister's room. When I walked inside, I was in for a surprise when I saw Max in there talking to Khloe like he's not the reason that she was in here the first place.

"Keri look who came to visit," Khloe announced as soon as I walked in the room.

"I see," I replied with a fake smile.

I walked over and kissed her on the cheek and just looked at Max like he was crazy for even showing his face.

"Keri," He spoke as he tried to place a kiss on my cheek but I moved my head.

"Don't you dare," I spoke in a harsh whisper.

He looked at me like he wanted to say more, but he wouldn't do it here in front of Khloe.

"So, you ready to go home?" I asked ignoring the looks that Max was giving me right now.

"Yes, I can't wait to finally get out of here and get a full night's sleep," She said smiling at me.

"Good, here's your stuff take it in the bathroom and shower and get dressed so we can head on out," I told her handing her the bag of clothes I bought.

When she walked in the bathroom and closed the door, I went off.

"What the fuck are you doing here Max?" I asked through gritted teeth.

"I came to bring you guys home," He spoke like shit was good between us.

"Excuse me?" I asked looking at him like he was stupid.

"I know I fucked up Keri, but I apologize and I don't want to lose you," He came with this dry ass apology; the funny thing was though was that he was serious.

"Max, we aren't coming back to your house, you hurt Khloe and I for the last time, so say your goodbyes and leave us the fuck alone," I threatened.

"I'm sorry I can't do that, I love you too much just to let you walk away like this, we aren't over," He stated grabbing me by the arm.

"Let go of me, you're hurting me Max," I told him looking towards the bathroom door.

"Did you hear what I said Keri? You and Khloe will be coming home when y'all leave from here. Do I make myself clear?"

"Crystal, in fact I can see right through you," I responded yanking my arm from his grip.

Before he had a chance to reply Khloe came from out the bathroom.

"I'm ready," She spoke with a smile.

"Good, I already asked the nurse for your discharge papers so we should be leaving out of here soon," I told her.

"Did I interrupt something here?" She asked looking between the both of us.

"Nope. Nothing at all," I replied with a smile.

I looked over at Max and he was texting away on his phone. I only hope he was getting called away for a meeting or something because he was starting to piss me off. I started getting her stuff ready and cleaning up a little before the nurse came in.

"Listen Khloe, they need me in the office right quick to sign some papers. I'll see you later at home," He told her as he hugged her.

"Oh okay, thanks for coming up here though," She replied hugging him back.

This whole situation was making my ass itch. I hated Max with a passion and I couldn't wait until he left and he was out of our lives for good.

"Keri, I'll see you at home," He stated with a serious look on his face.

"Yup," Was all I had to say, I don't know why he didn't believe what the fuck I told him. Khloe and I weren't going to be there when he gets home, but I guess I can show him better than I can tell him.

He smiled at the both of us then turned and walked out the hospital room and I released the breath that I was holding. I was so happy that he was gone so that I could finally talk to my sister alone.

"Listen Khloe we aren't going back to the house tonight," I started to explain.

"What? Wait, why not, what happened?" She asked all confused.

"A lot," Was all I said.

"Keri, I know you're my big sister and stuff but I'm old enough to know what's going on especially if it affects my life also," She stated.

I looked at her and that's when I realized that my sissy was growing up, she was old enough to know what was going on.

"Okay, you're right. I'll tell you what's up when we leave here," I told her.

"Okay, thank you Keri… for everything," She told me.

"Don't mention it, you know I got you… for life," I stated squeezing her hand with a smile.

"Hello ladies," The doctor walked in wearing a smile.

"Hi," Khloe responded.

"Doctor,"

"Doctor," She responded back with a head nod and a smile.

"Are those my discharge papers in your hand?" Khloe asked anxiously making us both laugh.

"Yes, ma'am these are them," She replied.

"Yaaaaaay," Khloe clapped.

The doctor spoke to Khloe and let her know that everything was all good, with her latest test results, but she needs to come back in within a month just for a follow-up.

"I can do that, thank you so much," She smiled shaking her hand.

"Anytime, see you soon," She replied handing Khloe her papers before walking out the room.

"You ready to go?" I asked.

"More then you know," She sang.

I grabbed her stuff and we both walked out the hospital, hopefully this would be the last time she would be here. We got into the car and I pulled off headed to Cree's house, the drive was quiet, my mind was all over the place. I knew that today wasn't going to be the last I saw of Max, so I was mentally preparing myself for that situation again.

"So, what's going on Keri?" Khloe asked wasting no time trying to find out what was going on.

I took a deep breath and tried to figure out the best way to tell her what was going on, she wanted to know so I just decided to tell her everything from the beginning. I let her know about Max abusing me and the reason why I stayed for so long. I let her know that Max was the reason why she ended up in the hospital and was always sick. By the time I was done with everything, she had tears coming down her face.

"I'm so sorry that you had to put up with all that behind me," She cried.

"Don't cry Khloe, your my sister I did what I had to do to make sure you were good. I'd do it again in a heartbeat if it meant I had to save your life," I told her honestly with a smile.

"Why didn't you tell me?"

"Tell you for what I'm grown and knew what I was getting myself into when I chose to stay," I admitted.

"I still can't believe he was keeping me sick to keep control over you, what kind of sick person does something like that?" She questioned.

"A really sick person, which is why we aren't going back there. We are going to stay with Cree until I find us a new place which should be by the end the week," I told her.

She nodded her head up and down as I told her what the next move was going to be, I know that she was dealing with a lot right now so I didn't want to overload her with it but she asked for it so I told her what it was.

Pulling up to Cree's, I parked the car and turned to look at Khloe, she was silent the whole ride to the house after I told her the truth,

"Hey, you good?"

She just nodded her head didn't even say anything, I left it alone for now but later I would be coming back to question her again. We both got out the car and I grabbed the suitcases that I had in the trunk and we walked up the steps to Cree's door. I used my key to get in her house. I really missed my best friend, this was the longest we have ever gone without talking and it was frustrating. We walked into her house and all of a sudden something wasn't right.

"Hold on Khloe," I told her stopping her at the front hall.

"What?"

"Just wait something isn't right here," I told her walking further in the house.

I heard a television on but I know that was impossible because last time I heard from Cobain, Cree was being held somewhere and I just know that if she was out he would have told me or better yet she would have called me herself.

I walked up the stairs to where I heard the noise and tried to see where it was coming from. I walked closer to her bedroom and saw that her door was on the floor which was making me a little more paranoid. I stopped and took a deep breath and walked into her room.

"What the fuck?!"

Chapter 21- Cree

"Oh my God bitch you scared the fuck out of me," I yelled grabbing my chest.

"Me? No, you scared the shit out of me and what the fuck are you doing here?" Keri asked walking into her room.

"Um I do live here; fuck kind of question is that?" I asked.

"Last time I heard your ass was kidnapped somewhere and I was waiting to hear from someone about your safe return," She stated folding my arms across my chest.

"Oh yeah that,"

"Oh yeah that," She replied mocking me.

"Stop, I'm sorry a lot happened and I honestly forgot to call you. But wait how did you know?" I asked with a confused look.

"Cobain told me," She said shrugging her shoulders.

"Should have known, wait what are you doing here?" I questioned looking at her strange.

"Wait before we get into all that give me a hug I missed youuuuuuu," I said pulling her into me.

"Oh my God bitch I missed you too, I've been going through hell," She told me hugging me back.

"We have a lot of catching up to do," I told her.

"Keri, you okay?" Khloe called out from downstairs.

"Oh, shit I forgot she was down there," She laughed walking out the room.

Keri went back downstairs to get Khloe while I followed behind her.

"Um what's all of this?" I asked pointing to the luggage.

"Were staying here for a while," She told me shrugging my shoulders.

"Oh yes, we definitely need to catch up," I replied rolling my eyes.

"Hey Cree," Khloe spoke.

"Hey babe, you looking good," I said with a smile.

"Khloe take your stuff up to the guest bedroom, I'll order some Chinese for you and I'll call you down when it's here," Keri spoke.

"Okay," She responded.

We both watched as she grabbed her luggage and went upstairs like I asked. Once she was out of sight, Cree started with the questions. She couldn't wait until to find out what was going on.

"Spill it bitch," I said pulling her into the kitchen.

"Nah you first how the fuck you get kidnapped?" She questioned.

I went and grabbed a bottle of wine out the fridge and two glasses and poured us both one and took the whole glass back and refilled it again before I started telling her what happened to me. She sat there listening to every detail of what I had to go through over them days I was gone.

"Damn girl," Was all she was able to get out before drinking her wine.

"Damn is right," I replied shaking her head.

"Where's Ali?" She asked.

"I don't know, I told him I didn't want to fuck with him,"

"Nooooo, really?" She laughed.

"Hell the fuck yeah, I don't have time to be looking over my shoulder every day of my life," I stated truthfully.

"How did he take that when you told him?" She asked.

I looked at her like she just asked the dumbest question in the world.

"What bitch?" She asked still confused as to why she was looking at me like that.

"That nigga gave me the best dick of my life that's what the fuck he did," I admitted putting her head down.

"Wait back up what?" She asked laughing.

"Bitch you heard what the fuck I said, he gave me the best dick and I still put him out" I fake sobbed.

"Oh my God I can't believe you," She said still laughing.

"I knooooooow,"

"Is he the reason your door was on the floor?" She asked.

"Yeah, he shot the shit down when I didn't open it for him to talk to me," I said shaking my head.

"That nigga is crazy over you," She told me still cracking up.

"Shut the fuck up, now what's going on with you and why you not at the palace," I asked as I poured myself another glass of wine.

"You got anything stronger then this wine? Because I'm going to need it for me to tell you this story," She asked.

"Yeah hold on I got some Grey Goose in the cabinet," I said pointing behind her.

She stood up off the stool and went to the cabinet and grabbed the bottle along with some juice I had in the fridge. She sat back down and poured herself a real drink and began telling me her horror story. She started from the top and told her everything leaving nothing out, by the time she was done my whole mouth was dropped.

"What the fuck is wrong with that nigga? To really stoop that low just to keep you nah, that's crazy," I said visibly pissed off.

"Girl, who you telling when he told me I wanted to kill him myself," She admitted.

"I can't even imagine how you felt hearing that shit, man if I was you I would let Cobain kill him. Who the fuck do he think he is beating you like he yo damn daddy?" I stated.

"I know, oh shit speaking of Cobain, I didn't even tell you what his baby mama done pulled,"

"Girl this is too much," I fanned myself.

"Tell me about it," She said shaking my head then finishing off my drink.

She started telling me about how she came to the house with the gun on her mad black woman shit and tried to kill us but ended up shooting herself.

"Stupid bitch, you want to fuck her up when she come out the hospital?" I asked but I was dead ass serious.

"Nah its good, she got her karma when she shot herself, so I aint even worried about her," She said.

"Shit me, what gives her the right to act like that because her nigga don't want her. She better be lucky I aint you because I would have pulled my petty card real fast and been like bitch you mad because your nigga and your kid love me," I stated in a matter of fact tone.

"Oh my God, you are stupid as fuck" She busted out laughing.

"Do not play with me, I can go from bougie to petty in the blink of an eye," I told her.

"Oh, I know, I've witnessed petty Cree and she isn't nothing to play with," She laughed.

"So, where's Cobain?"

"I don't know, we got into it and I haven't seen him since walking out on him," She admitted.

"Well what the fuck he do? I asked.

She began telling me about the shit he said to her when she had stayed at his house and all I could do was shake my head. I mean he was right, but I'm sure his approach was all wrong, niggas didn't know how to be subtle.

"Wow."

"Wow that's all you have to say Cree?" She asked.

"I mean-,"

"Fuck you, Cree," She said so harshly.

"Damn bitch I felt that fuck you in my spirit, you really meant that shit huh?" I asked trying to hold in my laugh.

"I swear I hate you," She said laughing first making me let go of the laugh I was holding.

"What are the odds of both of ending up dealing with crazy ass niggas?" I asked still in shock behind it.

"Um I don't have a crazy nigga that's all you boo," She stated with a smirk.

"Man, whatever Cobain crazy as fuck too, mark my words. They roll in packs like that, have you heard from him?" I asked giving her the side eye.

"Nope block game strong," She said sticking her tongue out at me.

"You stupid as fuck, but I missed the fuck out of you," She admitted as she squeezed my hand.

"I forgot you are an emotional drunk," I joked taking her glass from her.

"Whatever, I'm going to lay down,"

"You know you forgot to order Khloe's her food right?" I reminded her.

"Oh shit, well if you remembered why the fuck didn't you do it then?" She asked as she covered her mouth with her hand.

"I thought you wasn't doing it anymore, and I figured she fell asleep since she didn't come down and ask for it," I shrugged.

"My head starting to hurt I'm going to lay on the couch," She said getting up from the table and walking out.

I got up and put our glasses in the sink and closed the rest of the bottle, then hit the lights and walked out the kitchen. I walked into the living room and Keri was already knocked out with her lightly snoring with her mouth open. I grabbed a throw blanket and covered her up and went upstairs. I stopped and checked on Khloe and she was also knocked out which I suspected. I closed the door and went to my room and got in my bed.

***

I woke up this morning with my door being banged on like it was the fuckin' police. I jumped up out of bed and went straight downstairs and swung the door open.

"WHY THE FUCK ARE YOU KNOCKING ON MY DOOR LIKE YOU CRAZY AT 7 IN THE MORNING?" I yelled at the man that was there scaring the hell out of him.

"Um I'm sorry ma'am, I was told to knock like that," He told me reading his notepad.

"Who the fuck told you to knock on my door like it was a fuckin' emergency?" I asked putting my hands on my hip.

"It was a Mr. Ali Thomas," He said reading his notes.

"Ali? Why the fuck are you here?' I asked getting pissed off.

"He hired me to fix your door, he said you were having problems with it," He spoke.

"Hmph I bet."

I opened the door further and allowed him to enter my house so he could fix my door. I was going to curse this nigga the fuck out for pulling this shit.

"Oh yeah he asked me to give you this," He stopped and said handing me a cell phone then continued on up the stairs to my room.

I took the cell and just looked at it, Ali was really something else. I shook my head and went in the kitchen to make myself a cup of coffee, jumping up like that gave me an instant headache. I put the cell on the counter and grabbed the stuff I was going to need.

"Good morning," Keri spoke walking into the kitchen.

"Good morning, I'm surprised you're up this early."

"That man fixing the door woke me up with all that drilling in shit, and why the fuck you didn't wake me up when you went upstairs? I woke up feeling like I was in the dam Twilight Zone, forgot where the fuck I was for a moment," She said making me laugh.

"You were looking so peaceful I didn't want to wake you," I explained.

She flipped me off and sat down at the table picking up the cell phone box.

"New phone, who dis?" She joked.

"You're so damn corny," I laughed.

"Whatever, where this come from?" She asked as she took it out the box.

That's when I told her all about the handyman coming to fix my door and him giving me the phone courtesy of Ali.

"Okay bitch let me find out you got the juice."

"Shut the fuck up please, I swear the older we get the cornier your jokes get," I remarked giving her the side eye.

I made us both a cup of coffee while she sat there and opened the phone box. She powered it on to program it for me to only find out that he did it already.

"Sooooo, it's already set up," She said with a smirk.

"Really?"

"Yup and he even texted you," She said laughing.

"Shut up," I yelled grabbing the phone from her hands.

Future: *I hope you like your wakeup call this morning; I knew you would get a kick out of it. lol. That's just a little payback for how you left me. (smirk emoji) so besides your door being fixed and your new phone thnx to me now you owe me so be ready later at 7pm.*

"Well what does it say?" Keri nosey ass yelled.

I just handed her the phone and let her read it for herself she looked up at me and has the craziest look on her face.

"Awwwww oh my God Cree, that was so sweet, are you going?" She inquired looking at me.

"I don't know."

"What the fuck you mean you don't know, reading between the lines it looks like you didn't really have much of a choice in the matter," She acknowledged.

"I am my own person and do what I please."

"Yeah okay, so you need me to help you find something to wear later?" I asked biting my bottom lip.

"Yeah," I laughed covering my face from embarrassment.

"I thought so," She laughed.

We both laughed and drank our coffee and talked shit while the man was putting in her new door, a little while later Khloe came down and we ended up making breakfast as we just continued with our girl talk. Even though I was enjoying my time with my girl, I couldn't wait until later when I saw Ali, I was actually missing him more then I wanted to admit.

Chapter 22- Cobain

I knew what Shyne was trying to do but I wasn't falling for the shit, all this cooking dinner and being helpful around the house was really starting to make me regret my decision to let her stay here. I don't understand why she just couldn't stay, heal, and go the hell on with her business and stop trying to fix something that isn't broken.

Today was a rare day where I didn't have shit to do so I planned on staying in and enjoying my alone time. This shit rarely happens so I was about to enjoy it to the fullest, the fridge in my man cave was stocked with beer. I had my blunts rolled up and the television was set on *Game Of Thrones*. I've been missing the season so I was about to get caught up while I could.

I didn't really do junk food but I had a weakness for anything red velvet, so I had some cupcakes down there that I kept in the stash for emergencies like today. Kaylee was in her room watching Frozen for the millionth time so I was good; she would watch that shit all day if you let her. Shyne was in her room gossiping with her annoying ass cousin, as usual.

I went in my man cave and closed the door behind me and picked up my other phone and shot Keri another text that I knew she was going to possibly ignore again but I didn't care.

Me: Keri don't make me bring you home where you belong, I'm tired of the games now!

I put the phone down on the table next to me and pressed play on the play on the television. I lit a blunt so I could really relax while watching my show; this is what I enjoyed most time to myself. No business, no drama, just me time. I wish I was out with Keri but she was still playing games with me. Once I got her back I was going to ignore the fuck out of her and see how she likes it.

She was the type woman I could see myself with long term and would be a great role model for Kaylee. I wasn't too worried though because she was going to be mine real soon, whether she knew it or not.

After about three hours of the show and a few more blunts and a shot or four, my eyes were starting to feel a little heavy. I decided to take a nap, I went and laid on the bed that I had down here for times like this. I laid down and dozed right off with Keri on my mind.

"What are we doing here?" I asked rubbing my eyes.

"Chilling, come on," He said getting out the car.

I opened my door and got out the car and walked over to him while he held his hand out for me. I grabbed his hand and he pulled me close to him as we stated walking towards the boardwalk. The walk to the boardwalk was quiet at first and I was just enjoying being around him.

"So, Ms. Keri tell me what's on your mind, and before you lie and say nothing don't, I can read people very well and I'll know that you are lying and I don't like liars," He stated.

"I'm just thinking about life, all the shoulda, coulda, and wouldas, all the what if's," I admitted.

"Do you have any regrets?" He inquired.

"Yes and no, but the things I regret are just lessons learned," I spoke looking up at him.

"Interesting. I won't ask you about your regrets... not yet anyway but one day," He added.

"Do you have any regrets?" I threw back at him.

"Honestly... no I don't. I live my life how I want and everything I do is my choice," He spoke.

"Must be nice," I mumbled.

"Huh?" He asked.

"Oh nothing," I replied with a light smile.

We continued to walk and talk asking questions to each other back and forth, until we felt like we knew enough about at this moment.

"You're a very interesting man Mr. Wade," I stated.

"I hope that's a good thing," He replied.

"It could be," I laughed.

"Real shit doc, I know you have a situation at home but I'm feeling the fuck out of you, it's just something about you that I can't seem shake. I wake up in the morning just wanting to be in your presence even if it's just to watch you work," He admitted.

"Wow, I don't even know what to say," I spoke.

"Its cool doc, you don't have to say anything I just wanted to tell you what was on my mind," He added.

We walked a little further in silence both of us lost in our thoughts, once we got to the end of the boardwalk we looked over at the waves and just stood there.

"It's so peaceful out here," I spoke breaking the silence.

"Doc," He called out.

"Yes?" I replied looking at him.

He looked me in my eyes and grabbed the side of my face with his hand and caressed it then leaned down and kissed me. I haven't been kissed like this in so long; I reached up and put my arms around him as he passionately kissed me like it was our last *time seeing each other. I pulled away and I don't know what came over me but I thought I should tell him about Max and I's relationship status.*

"*I'm leaving my fiancé,*" *I admitted.*

"*What? Are you serious?*" *He questioned.*

"*Yes,*" *I replied shaking my head up and down.*

He picked me up and spun me around as he continued to kiss me all over my face.

"*You just made my night doc,*" *He said in between kisses causing me to throw my head back in laughter.*

Hearing her laughter in my head made me jump up from my nap. I needed to see her now and that what I was about to do, I didn't want to be without her as a part of my life for another day. I walked of my cave and went to my room to shower so I could go pull up on Keri and let her know that her time was up and she had no say in the matter.

I took a quick shower and through on my joggers and a shirt with some Nike's. I grabbed my fitted throwing it on before I walked out my room and stopped and checked on Kaylee before I left out the house.

"Hey baby girl," I announced walking into her room.

"Hi daddy, mommy said you were in your man room and I couldn't bother you," She said taking a quick glance at me before returning her eyes back to the television.

"I was but you are always welcome wherever I'm at," I stated.

"Okay daddy," She replied with a smile.

"I just came to check on you before I head out," I told her.

"Oh, where are you going can I go with you?" She asked giving me the puppy dog eyes.

"Not this time Kaylee, but next time I got you, you can ride passenger side," I bribed.

"I guess that's fine daddy," She fake pouted.

"Don't do that, you know if I could I would, but I just need to take care of something and I'm coming right back then me and you can hang," I suggested to her making her face light up.

"Yaaay okay daddy, go and hurry back," She said pushing me off her bed.

"You are something else," I laughed.

"Hurry daddy."

I walked out her room and went downstairs where I heard some arguing going on but I know that couldn't be right because nobody would come to my house and who the fuck would Shyne be arguing with. The closer I got down the steps the voices got clearer and I recognized that voice anywhere, and I knew I had just fucked up.

I walked up to the door and saw Keri, Cree and Shyne having a heated argument. I knew this wasn't going to be good. When I got to the door Keri and I locked eyes and she had this look of disappointment on her face.

"Doc, what are you doing here?" I asked.

"I just came to drop your car off and maybe talk to you, but it's cool," She replied handing me my keys before she started to walk off.

"Doc wait," I called out,

"Why? You're busy with your family. I don't want to interrupt your family time," She told me.

"Keri, you sure you don't want me to slap her? I still owe her one for pulling a gun out on you," Cree called out.

"Bitch I wish you would," She replied.

"I got your bitch just give me a reason, I have a lot of pent of frustrations and I would love to take it out on your face," She stated in a matter of fact tone.

"Cree let's go she's not worth it," I replied.

"Doc it's not even like that. I don't know what she told you but none of it is true," I tried to tell her.

"She said she was living back with you and y'all was trying to make your family work, even if it isn't true the fact that she is still here after she tried to shoot us tells me a lot about you. I just came out of something toxic and I won't be in another one," She explained getting in the car.

"You better control your pit bull in a skirt next time I'm going to reach out and touch her rude ass," Cree said getting in the car and pulling off.

I looked at the car as it was pulling off and I felt my blood pressure rising, I turned and looked at Shyne and she stood there like a deer caught in headlights. I walked into the house slamming the door behind me.

"WHAT THE FUCK DID YOU DO? WHY WOULD YOU TELL HER THAT SHIT FOR?" I asked backing her into a corner.

"I didn't tell her anything that wasn't true Cobain, I'm here because you allowed me into your home-"

"UNTIL YOU WERE WELL ENOUGH TO TAKE CARE OF YOURSELF, THAT'S THE ONLY REASON," I yelled.

"Cobain, things here have been going good, I just assumed that you felt the same way."

"You know what they say about people that assume shit right Shyne? I don't know why you would assume that when I told you that we will NEVER be together. Why can't you understand that shit? I let you stay with me because you are the mother of my child and this is how you replay me?"

"Cobain,"

"Save it, you have to go now, and when I say now I mean RIGHT NOW," I told her as I walked away.

"Please don't do this," She cried.

"Save them tears for somebody who cares because I don't, and the little bit of affection I had for you, you just fucked that up. Be gone when I get back Shyne," I ordered walking out the house.

I got in my car and pulled out my driveway. I didn't have a destination in mind but I needed to get out that house before I caught a murder charge with my kid upstairs. I kept calling Keri's phone but she was sending me to voicemail. I didn't like the look she gave me when she left, I knew I had a lot of explaining to do. I just hope she gave me the opportunity to do it.

Chapter 23- Keri

I can't believe Cobain right now, I was so mad with him. I can't believe he led me on the way he did only for him to lie to me.

"Keri, you good?"

"Yes… no," I admitted.

"Don't let that shit get to you girl," She said trying to cheer me up.

"Easier said than done Cree. I know I may not have shown it but I was really feeling him, it's just that life got in the way and I couldn't act on my feelings," I told her.

"Ohhhhhhhh, got it,"

"Like I don't get it, she tried to kill us why are they playing house?" I asked myself more than Cree.

"Listen sis you might not want to hear this, but I'm on the outside looking in so don't shoot the messenger," She said glancing at me.

"Okay," I replied not really knowing if I really wanted to hear what she was about to say.

"Here's the real, at the end of the day Cobain is a man and baby they don't really know any better. He probably let her stay there while she got better, -"

"But WHY? It's her own damn fault that she was injured in the first place." She stated interrupting me.

"Bitch I get that your mad but interrupt me again and I'm going to pull this car over and fuck you up," I threatened.

"Sorry," She apologized.

"Thank you, now as I was saying, at the end of the day that's still his kid's mother, and when she's good his daughter will be good. So maybe he thought it would be a good idea to help her recover faster and keep his daughter from being neglected or something," I explained.

"I guess, it makes sense but still, whyyyyyyyyyy," I called out.

"Listen this is the shit you have to deal with sometimes when you deal with a man that has a baby mama that has no damn sense. If you like him like you say you do then talk to him and see what's up, I guarantee you that it isn't what you think," She explained.

"How do you know?" I asked.

"Because the look of death he gave her when you told him what she said, told me otherwise," She stated.

"I'll see how I feel later, I just need time to think about what I want to do next," I told her.

"Cool with me, but the way he was looking at you he's not waiting for you much longer," She told me in a matter of fact tone of voice.

I didn't even bother to respond to her because deep down I knew she was right. I just needed to figure out if I really wanted to deal with this for the rest of my life. The rest of the ride was a silent one. As soon as we pulled up to the house Ali was pulling up at the same time.

"There goes your babyyyyyyyyyy," I sang out in my best Usher voice.

"I know," Cree said blushing, she's been doing that a lot since meeting Ali. I was so happy she gave him a chance she deserved all this that she was getting.

We both got out the car and she walked up to Ali and wrapped her arms around him as he did the same.

"What's up doc," He greeted.

"Hey Ali, good to see you again," I replied walking up the stairs.

"Hey doc?"

"Yes," I turned and replied.

"That shit that just went down, it wasn't even like what she said it was. She is miserable and he don't want her ass," He told me.

"Okay,"

"I'm not just saying that because he's my bro, I'm keeping it real. If you really want to know I told him not to let her stay with him, but he does shit to keep Kaylee happy," He explained.

"Thank you," I smiled.

"Also, he's coming to get you, so be ready and he's not taking no for an answer," He added with a smile.

"Keri, I'll be back later," Cree announced.

"Okay," I responded walking into the house.

I closed the door behind me and went and sat in the living room and just laid my head back on the couch. My mind was so clouded that I didn't know what to do anymore, I know a vacation was coming real soon.

I heard a knock at the door and opened my eyes, maybe Cree forgot her keys.

"You forgot something?" I yelled jogging to the door opening it to see Max standing there.

"What the fuck are you doing here?" I asked.

He walked past me into the house without saying anything to me; I took a deep breath and counted to ten. I was not in the mood for his shit today.

"Max what are you doing here?" I asked again.

"Why do you think I'm here Keri? Why the fuck haven't you brought your ass home yet and better yet why the fuck did you destroy all my things?" He asked through gritted teeth walking up to me slamming the door.

"I told you that the you and I were done when we were at the hospital Max, you chose to ignore me. That house belongs to you not me, Khloe and I don't live there anymore," I stated.

"I know that I told you we will never be over; the only way we will ever be apart is if one of us is dead. I've invested a lot of money into you and your family and I'll be damned if I let you just walk away like that," He threatened getting closer to my face.

He was so close that I could smell the alcohol on his breath and it was making me nauseous.

"Max, you need to go," I told him, I was over this whole conversation and I wasn't about to be repeating myself over and over like I was talking to a toddler.

"Did you hear what the fuck I said Keri?" He asked grabbing me by the neck and choking me.

I grabbed his wrist and started scratching at his arms and wrist as he squeezed harder cutting off my air circulation.

"Max let me go," I managed to get out.

"You see how easy it would be for me to kill you right here Keri, why do you continue to make me put my hands on you? Why can't you just listen when I talk to you?" He asked squeezing harder.

I felt myself losing consciousness quickly, I looked him in the eyes as he continued to squeeze my neck and it wasn't him I was looking at. He looked like a completely different person. He finally let me go and I dropped to the floor and started dry coughing and gasping for air.

"Stop fuckin with me Keri or Khloe will be burying her big sister," He threatened.

I looked at him with so much hate in my eyes at that moment that if I had a gun I would shoot him in the head right now.

"I'm sending someone by later to pick you and Khloe up and you better be ready to come home," He stated.

I didn't respond I just rubbed my neck looking at him.

"Don't make me hurt you Keri," He said bending down and trying to kiss me.

I turned my head so his lips wouldn't touch me.

"Believe it or not Keri I love you… to death," He said before he walked out the house.

I slowly got up off the floor and locked the door. I was just so happy that Khloe wasn't here to see this. I went and looked in the mirror at my neck, it wasn't bad yet but I knew it wouldn't take long for my neck to be bruised up. I looked at myself in the mirror long enough that I broke down cry, I just couldn't catch a break and it was all becoming too much for me to handle.

I went and laid down on the couch, I just needed a minute to get myself together and figure out my next move. It was time for Khloe and I to move into our own spot and fast. As soon as I get up from my nap I was going to contact my realtor and find me a place today.

***

I woke to the door being knocked on and I immediately got startled, thinking it was whoever the hell Max said he was going to have come get mine and Khloe's stuff. I didn't answer, but I saw Khloe coming down the steps to answer the door.

"Khloe wait," I jumped up but it was too late she already answered it.

When I got to the door I saw that it was Cobain and his daughter, which shocked me. Khloe looked at me and I nodded my head for her to let them in. When he walked in the smile on his face instantly disappeared and I didn't understand why until I saw his eyes focused on my neck and that's when I remembered what happened earlier. I quickly excused myself and went to my room and threw on a hoodie. I walked back into the living room where Cobain had the look of death in his eyes.

"Hello, who is this pretty girl?" I asked looking at his daughter.

"I'm Kaylee, his daughter," She replied with a smile as she leaned into him.

"Well it's very nice to meet you Kaylee, my name is Keri," I introduced holding my hand out for her to shake it.

"It's nice to meet you too, you're very pretty," She giggled.

"Why thank you Kaylee, your very pretty yourself," I acknowledged.

"Thank you, my daddy calls me pretty girl," She admitted.

"That's a very fitting name for you," I winked.

She smiled at me as we talked and I couldn't help but be drawn to her.

"What are you doing here?" I asked Cobain.

"I came to talk but I don't know if that's a good idea anymore," He stated.

"My daddy said that you were mad at him, so he brought me with him so I can make you happy again so you won't be mad at him anymore," Kaylee admitted.

"Oh, did he?" I laughed.

"He did, can you please not be mad at my daddy anymore. Whatever he did he didn't mean it, and besides you know boys are always doing something bad, the ones in my class are always in trouble," She said whispering that last part to me so Cobain wouldn't hear making me literally laugh out loud.

"Can I talk to you for a minute please?" Cobain interrupted us standing up and walking into the kitchen not even giving me the chance to respond.

"Kaylee do you want to watch television while I talk to your dad?" I asked.

"Yes please."

I turned the television on and found a kid friendly movie that she could watch while I talked to her dad. After I found something for her to watch I walked into the kitchen and stood away from Cobain, the way he was looking he was probably liable to snap.

"What's up?" I asked.

"What the fuck happened to your neck Keri? He asked getting straight to the point.

"Cobain,"

"Don't lie, now tell me what the fuck happened to your neck?" He asked in a harsh whisper.

I took a deep breath and told him about Max and his pop up visit at the house earlier. After I was done I waited to see what he was going to say, he didn't say anything at first and it had me on pins and needles.

"First, I'm going to take care of that nigga Max so you don't even worry about him anymore," He started saying.

"Cobain no, it's fine. I can handle it," I tried to tell him.

"Doc chill, I got this already. Second, I need to apologize to you for what happened at my house earlier, as a man I feel fucked up for what went down. I thought I could help her out since she was the mother of my child but I see I can't even be nice to her like that. I never want to put you in a position where you can't trust me or have to second guess anything when it comes to me," He explained.

"Thank you,"

"Third from this day forward you are my woman. I'm not playing these games with you anymore. I tried to give you time to come around on your own but you never got the memo of our relationship, so I'm here to help you out," He stated.

"Just like that?" I asked.

"Just like that, I tried to wait for you to come on your own but you kept getting side tracked and blocking me," He joked.

"I hear you," I laughed.

"Keri look at me, I'm serious. I want you. I've wanted you from the first day I laid eyes on you in the hospital and I told Ali I would have you and I always get what I want," He stated walking up to me and standing in front of me.

"Is that so?" I asked as I bit my bottom lip.

"It is," He replied leaning down to kiss me. I reached up and wrapped my arms around his neck and kissed him back.

I've waited a long time to kiss him again, and this kiss was better than I remembered. Once we pulled away he just stared at me then kissed me on the tip of my nose.

"Let's go before Kaylee comes in here poppin shit, she's very territorial of me," He laughed.

"Oh, I can imagine especially if she's anything like her mama," I teased walking out the kitchen laughing.

"To soon," He spoke slapping me on the ass.

We both walked back into the living room and sat and watched the rest of the movie with Kaylee. After it was over we ordered food and just hung out in the living room. Khloe and Kaylee got along well you wouldn't even know that it was their first time meeting each other. Kaylee stayed under Khloe, it was actually really cute to see, it's like she enjoyed having somewhat of a big sister around.

For the first time in a long time my life actually felt normal, I was at peace and I owed it all to Cobain and Kaylee. This was a life that I could get used to, I looked over at Cobain the same time he looked at me and he winked at me, instantly giving me butterflies.

Chapter 24- Ali

I was waiting for Cree to text me back but knowing her stubborn ass she wasn't going to but it was cool as long as she showed her ass up tonight I wouldn't pop up on her. I was actually nervous as fuck about this date tonight; I didn't even know what I was doing. I just knew I wasn't going to be without her anymore and tonight she will know.

Cobain and I were in the mall picking up a few things, I already knew what I was wearing I just needed to pick up a fresh pair of kicks and a new bottle of cologne.

"So, what's the plan for Cree tonight?" Cobain asked as we walked inside of Jimmy Jazz.

"Truthfully bro I don't know, I'm thinking of what I want to do but nothing seems good enough, I need for her to really be feeling this so I can get her back," I said as I walked over to the sneaker wall.

"Them Nike's are hard, you fuckin' with those?"

"I might, they go with my outfit so maybe," I replied looking at them.

"So, you know what you wearing but not where you going? How does that work?" He laughed.

"I don't know man, I was just going with the flow," I stated.

"I see that," He chuckled.

"Man whatever, I'll figure it out I still have a few hours until I have to pick her up,"

"I think I have something you can do for her," Cobain announced.

"Well why the hell you just now saying something then?" I asked about to get pissed off with him.

"I like seeing you sweat," He joked.

"Fuck you, what's the plan?" I asked as I walked to the register to pay for my sneakers.

"Aight check it," He started to explain and I was all ears.

"My nigga I like that shit," I replied slapping him five.

"I knew you would, I already placed the call to my man so you already set up for tonight," He stated.

"You are the man for this one; I appreciate it for real bro. I know she's going to love that,"

"I'm sure she is," He replied.

We walked out the first store and walked into a jewelry store, I was just looking around for nothing in particular just wanted to see what they had that I might like.

"So, what's up with you and the doctor?" I asked picking his brain.

"Nothing is up, we just taking it slow at the moment, I told her she's mine already but I'm still trying to let her handle her situation on her own, but I already know I'm taking care of it for her, especially after what I saw last night," He stated in a matter of fact tone.

"What the fuck did you see?" I asked looking at him.

"Man, Kaylee and I went over there and she had marks all on her neck, I couldn't even focus on shit else that she was saying," He explained.

"Are you shitting me right now? What the fuck happened?" I barked.

He started telling me what she told him about Max poppin' up and threating her and choking her out.

"Nah he's buggin' and needs to be dealt with like right now," I stated.

"Trust me I know, I have something in the works now," He admitted.

"Well what is it nigga, stop holding out," I barked.

He started telling me about his plan and how he was going to handle Max, by the time he was done telling me his plan we both had smiles on our faces.

"My nigga," I smirked giving him a dap.

"Right," I chuckled.

"When is this going down?" I questioned.

"Sooner than you think," He winked.

"Ayo boss man, let me see this right here please," I called out to the worker.

"No problem sir," He replied walking over to me and opening the case up pulling the shelf out.

"That's nice as fuck bro, but why the fuck you looking at engagement rings for. I know you not about to do what I think you about to do," He inquired with a strange look on his face.

"Just mind your damn business you always in my shit bro," I replied shaking my head.

"This is a very nice ring sir. The cut and quality of the diamonds are one of a kind, you can't go wrong with this right here," He explained as he handed me the ring.

"Say my man how much this shit running for?" Cobain nosey ass had the nerve to ask the man even though he wasn't paying for shit.

"Don't tell this man shit, I'm the customer not him Saleem," I stated reading his nametag.

I continued to study the ring to see if I could see this on Cree's finger, it was beautiful but I wasn't sure if it was perfect enough for her.

"You studying that ring mighty hard bro and for the price that shit cost I'm sure she will love that shit," Cobain said breaking me from my thoughts.

"How the fuck you know what it cost?"

"Money talks, I gave him a big face and he told me what it cost," He said like that shit was normal.

"Can't take your ass nowhere I swear," I chuckled.

"Real shit though, you ready for this?" He asked seriously.

I looked him in the eyes and thought really hard before I answered him so he would know that I was serious.

"I'm ready bro, I haven't felt like this about another female since Ashanti, and now that I found it again I don't want to lose it," I told him honestly.

"Well in that case man I support you, you know what you want to get her and don't take no for an answer," He told me.

"That's the plan, thanks for the support. I should be telling you the same thing but I'll save that for another day," I chuckled.

"So, boss you taking it?" Saleem asked.

I looked at Cobain and he gave me the nod of approval and I turned and looked at Saleem and smiled.

"I'll take, wrap it up as a gift," I told him handing him back the ring.

"My man" Cobain said giving me dap.

***

I was on the way to Cree's house ready to pick her up for our date, I don't know why the fuck I was so nervous this wasn't even like me at all. That's how I know that what I was feeling for her was real. I had taken a shot before I left to calm my nerves, but it wasn't really doing shit for me.

I had pulled up to her house and instead of being my usual jackass self and honk the horn I decided to ring the bell to let her know that I was here. I took a breath and got out the car walked up to the door and rang the bell and waited for her to answer. After a few moments, I heard the door unlock and it opened up.

"Hey Ali," Keri spoke with a grin on her face.

"Wassup doc," I replied rubbing my hand across my mustache.

"Come in Cree is almost ready," She said opening the door letting me walk in.

"Thanks doc,"

I walked in and looked around and saw a girl that looked like a younger version of the doctor.

"Who is this?" I asked.

"Ali this is my little sister Khloe, Khloe this is Ali," She introduced us.

"Nice to meet you," She smiled.

"Likewise," I replied with a head nod.

"You looking real nice and dapper," Keri said.

"What the fuck is dapper doc?" I asked laughing.

"Shut up, it just means you look real clean and nice," She laughed flipping me the bird.

"My bad doc I kind of figured but wasn't really sure," I chuckled.

"Whatever let me go see if Cree is ready," She said rolling her eyes and walking away.

I sat and made myself comfortable on the couch while I waited for Keri to come back down with Cree. I kept tapping my pocket that held the ring in it; it became a habit now just making sure it was there.

"Hey Ali,"

I picked my head up and there was Cree looking like an African princess, she had on this burnt orange dress that was hugging her body in all the right places showing off her amazing figure. Shit I was about to be a lucky man.

"Are you going to stare at me all night or are you going to speak?" She asked breaking me from my X rated thoughts.

"My bad ma but damn, you look good as fuck right now," I told her truthfully making her chocolate skin blush.

"Thank you,"

I stood up and pulled her in for a hug and her scent instantly got my dick hard. I was definitely getting in them guts tonight.

"You ready?" I asked pulling away from her.

She nodded up and down, so I grabbed her hand and led her to the front door so we could leave.

"Y'all kids have fun now, but not too much fun. Ali make sure you have my girl here back at a decent hour," Keri yelled as we were getting in the car.

I saw Cree flip her off as she was getting in the car I just laughed and closed the door.

"Ali,"

"Wassup?" I responded.

"Take care of my girl," She stated seriously.

"I got her, trust me," I told her with a wink and I got inside the car.

I started the car and pulled off because I was on a time schedule and needed to get to the spot.

"Where are we going?" Cree asked.

"Just relax your mind and let your conscious breathe, your now rolling with the thug named Ali," I joked mimicking Jay-Z

"You're so corny," She laughed.

"Whatever you like it though."

"Who said that? And who the fuck told you I was going to actually be ready tonight?" She inquired.

"Nobody told me but I know you didn't want no static with me, so you jumped right on board with this date night shit, text or no text," I let her know straight up.

"Shut up, you don't know me," She replied rolling them damn eyes of hers.

"Keep rolling them eyes and they going to get stuck like that, didn't your mama ever teach you that growing up?" I asked taking my eyes off the road to look at her.

"Shut up, and the next time you bring her up I'm telling her, because you steady poppin' shit about how she raised me."

"Tell her I don't care. I'm not scared of your mama," I told her.

"You won't be saying that shit when Dorthey come step to you with that cane of hers, she don't play about hers," She laughed.

"I'll trip Dorthey's ass, fuck you talking about," I joked.

"So, where are we going?" She asked again thinking I forgot she already asked.

"It's a surprise sit back and enjoy the ride beautiful, I'm about to show you a whole new world," I looked at her and winked.

"Okay Aladdin, I hear that," She replied.

She sat back like I asked and enjoyed the ride; we had light conversation on the way there. I pulled up to the spot and parked the car I turned to look at her then spoke.

"Do you trust me?"

"What? Why? Where is all this coming from?" She asked all nervous.

"Ma chill, nothing like that but I need to know do you trust me?" I asked seriously.

I looked at her and waited for an answer, she looked like she wasn't really sure and it was crushing a nigga ego that she still wasn't trusting me. She looked at me and slowly nodded her head up and down.

"I can't hear you Cree; do you trust me?" I asked again.

"Yes, Ali I trust you damn man, now what's this all about?" She asked getting annoyed.

"You will see in a minute now let's go, get out the car," I told her as I got out on my side.

I stood by the hood of the car and waited for her to get out the car; once she did she walked over to me and stood next to me.

"What is this place?" She asked.

"You ask A LOT of questions did anyone ever tell you that?" I questioned grabbing her hand and kissing it.

"Yeah, all the time now tell me where we are," She stated.

"Come on let's go," I said leading her to the door of the building.

Once inside I pressed the button on the elevator and we stood there and waited for it to come. I took a look at Cree and she was still trying to figure out what was going on and I loved every minute of it. The elevator came and we both stepped on I pressed the button for us to go to the roof.

When we got to the top and stepped off the elevator I looked at Cree and waited for her reaction.

"Wait, we're getting on a helicopter?" She asked shocked.

"Yeah, I hope you're not scared of heights."

"Nope, I actually love heights," She said excitedly.

"Good, let's go," I grabbed her hand and led her to the helicopter.

"Ali my man," The pilot greeted.

"Billy what's good bro, we all good here?" I asked.

"For sure, just waiting on you," He said.

I held Cree's hand as she walked up the steps to board the helicopter then I followed behind her sitting next to her. We both buckled our seatbelts and waited for the pilot to get in and lift us up in the air.

"Oh my God Ali I'm so excited, I've always wanted to do this," She said with the biggest smile on her face.

"I'm glad I could do this for you, just seeing this smile on your face tells me it was worth it," I admitted.

The pilot started the helicopter and lifted it up off the ground; we both put the headset on that was provided. I held her hand as we got higher in the sky, her eyes never left from the view and my eyes never left from off her. My nerves were really getting the best of me and I decided to just propose to her now and just get it over with because I wasn't good with keeping stuff like this in for too long.

I waited a little longer until we got a little higher and over more skylights so I could make this a night she would always remember.

I pulled the ring out my pocket and opened the box all while still holding onto Cree's hand. She never once looked my way which I was thankful for; I held the ring on my lap and called out for her.

"Cree,"

"Huh?" She replied but still not looking at me.

"Cree," I called out again.

"Yes Ali, I'm admiring the vie-," She stopped mid-sentence gasping and covering her mouth.

"I got something I need to ask you."

"What are you doing?" She asked shaking.

"I had this big ol proposal planned out for you tonight, but watching you be excited over this and knowing that I could make you happy made me just do this now. I know I may not get this right but I'd rather try and mess up over and over with you then with anyone else. When I lost my ex I never in a million years thought that I would find love again, then I met you and even though at first, we didn't hit it off when we did it was amazing. When I thought I lost you, something in my mind and heart clicked and I knew that I never wanted to be apart from you ever again. That's when I knew you were the one for me, my heart cried thug tears when you were gone and I never want to feel like that again. I lost you once and I don't wanna lose you again, so I'm asking you over this beautiful NYC skyline and amazing background will you be my wife?"

I waited for her to respond but she was too busy wiping the tears that were falling.

"You don't even know my last name or my favorite color," She said through tears making me laugh.

"Minor details babe, but I have the rest of my life to get to know you if you say yes. So, what do you say Cree?" I asked again.

"YESSSSSSSSSSS," She yelled.

I took the ring out the box and placed it on her finger then kissed her like it was our last time.

"OH MY GOD, THIS IS BEAUTIFUL," She squealed.

"Only the best for you.

"Thank you, I can't wait for Keri to see this bad boy. You did really good," She smiled leaning over and kissing me again.

I saw her pull out her phone and take a picture of her ring then send a text message I'm sure it was to Keri, she couldn't wait for her to see it. No later than that text was sent did her phone ring. She answered it and put it on speaker.

"AHHHHHHHHHHHH OH MY GOD CREEEEEEEE," She screamed.

"Ayo doc, stop screaming like that," I told her.

"Shut up, I'm soooo happy for my girl, that ring is beautiful. You did good Ali," She said.

"Thank you, anything for Cree," I said truthfully making her blush as usual.

"Cree hurry up and come home so we can pop a bottle and celebrate and I can see that baby in person," She said excitedly.

"Bye doc," I said hanging up on her.

"Why did you do that?" She laughed.

"Because you on my time, you will talk to her later,"

"Okay," She replied putting her purse back in her bag.

"Pilot take us back to the building," I demanded.

"Yes sir,"

"Wait why?" She pouted.

"Because I'm ready to fuck my fiancé, I'll make it up to you, but between that smile and the way that dress fitting my dick is hard as fuck," I told her making her blush.

We made out like teenagers the whole way back to the landing pad, I couldn't wait to get her back to the crib and get her pregnant. Little did she know I had plans for her.

Chapter 25 - Max

I don't know why Keri always made shit difficult, I may have a funny way of showing it, but I did love her. My dad beat my mom all the time and she still stayed with him and they're still happily married, I was just following in his footsteps but Keri was doing everything all wrong.

I had to hire someone to come clean the house after the mess that Keri left it in here. I never expected her to leave her ring and keys behind. When I saw that I knew she was really done, but I thought I could get her back, but it's turning out to be a more difficult task then I imagined.

I heard my doorbell ring and I got excited, I just knew Keri would come to her senses and bring her ass home where she belongs it was only a matter of time. I went downstairs and opened the door only to be disappointed.

"Can I help you?" I asked the delivery man.

"Yes, I have a delivery for a Mr. Max glass," He announced looking at his clipboard.

"A delivery from whom?" I asked accepting the package.

"From a Mr. Grossam," He read.

"Hmm okay, that's strange," I mumbled to myself.

"Please sign here."

"Sure, thank you," I replied signing the paper and closing the door behind me. I walked in the kitchen and sat the package on the table.

I pulled the card that was on the front read it to myself.

"To the future"

I guess talking about our recent partnership with his company, he had no choice we both needed each other for different reasons. I dropped the card on the table and opened the package and saw that it was bottle of my favorite.

"My man," I chuckled.

I don't know how he knew but I'm very appreciative of this bottle. I went and grabbed a glass and popped open the bottle. I poured some in the glass and stirred the cup a little before taking it straight back. I swallowed the drink straight and poured me another glass taking that one back also.

After a few minutes, I started feeling funny, I immediately dropped the glass causing it to shatter on the ground, and my hands went straight to my neck. I don't know what was wrong but I was feeling funny all of a sudden.

"That right there is the poison that you're feeling coursing through your veins right now," I heard from behind me.

I turned around and saw it was the man that was in the picture with Keri from that night and my eyes got wider and I tried to speak but nothing came out.

"Arsenic is one hell of a poison, right now your body is paralyzing itself and you are slowly dying," He explained.

My eyes got even wider and I tried to make a run for it but nothing happened.

"Since I have you here, do you know why you're about to die?" He asked as if he was expecting an answer from me, so I nodded my head up and down.

"You are a coward of a man if you have to put your hands on a female to try and control them. Only pussies beat women. You don't get points for shit like that, you are the type of man that will fight a woman but run and press charges on a nigga like me if I ever stepped to you. You fucked up by putting your hands on Keri though. She's mine now and I'll be damned if you lay another finger on her ever again," He explained.

I dropped down on the floor and felt myself slowly dying on the inside.

"I could have shot you and made your death a lot quicker, but I needed you to understand why it is that you were dying. I just knew you would accept that bottle without any questions asked.

You made this shit too easy for me. Isn't it ironic that the drug of choice that you chose to indulge in everyday of your life is the same drug that is slowly killing you right now," He said laughing.

"Don't worry though Keri will be in good hands that is a promise," was the last thing I heard before I didn't hear shit anymore.

Chapter 26- Keri

I was packing up my stuff from Cree's place so that Khloe and I could finally move into our own place. It took a little longer then I wanted but it finally was happening, and I couldn't be any more excited. As much as I loved staying here with her, it was time for Khloe and I to have our own again. I found a nice house to rent in Jamaica Estates that was perfect for us.

"I don't want you to goooooooo, I love having y'all here," Cree walked in pouting sitting on the bed.

"Really? I couldn't tell since your ass isn't ever home anymore," I joked rolling my eyes.

"I know, I'm sorry Ali and I have just been getting reacquainted," She smiled.

"I know and it's cool, I'm so happy for you, especially with everything that has happened. You deserve your happily ever after," I told her seriously.

"Thank you, but so do you. Cobain is it for you," She stated.

"We shall see,"

"I don't know why you trying to play coy with me, you know you feeling the fuck out that man. Once you finally get some act right you going to be singing a different tune,' She laughed.

"Shut up," I laughed throwing a pillow at her.

"Nah but for real from what I got from Ali he's really feeling you, like since the first day he opened his eyes type of shit, you the one bihhhh," She told me seriously.

"I like him too, I just don't want to make the same mistakes twice-"

"He's not Max, so don't even go there," She said cutting me off.

"I know, I know,"

"Good, now let's go have a glass of wine to celebrate this new journey in both of our lives," She suggested.

"Wine, girl it's not even five yet,"

"It's 5 O'clock somewhere," She chuckled getting off the bed.

I got off the floor and grabbed my phone and followed her downstairs to the kitchen, soon as I walked in she was already poppin' the top off the bottle.

"Couldn't wait huh," I joked.

"Nope," She replied before she drank some from her glass making me laugh.

"You are something else,"

"But you love me though, so that's all that matters," She replied.

"Just a little," I sassed.

"Can you believe I'm really engaged Keri, who would have thought that after everything I been through I would becoming someone's wife," She spoke.

"I knew and I told you, just be patient and let it find you and look you did. You were so hurt behind Jameer that you were looking for love in all the wrong places and only finding yourself hurt even more, but you see what happened when you stopped and let it find you, I haven't seen you this happy in a long time," I admitted.

"I know, thank you for always sticking by me through all my mistakes and just through life, I love and appreciate you more then you will ever know," She told me sounding emotional.

"That's what I'm here for girl, till death do us part," I told her seriously.

"Till death," She reiterated.

"So, about this weeding how are we doing this?" I asked changing gears on the conversation.

"I kind of want a destination wedding but then again I don't know, I told him two years max time though. I don't want a long engagement,"

"I feel you, well I guess we have a wedding to plan," I yelled excitedly.

We were sitting there laughing and having a good time, talking about wedding stuff and my phone wouldn't stop ringing.

"Girl who is blowing you up you phone like that?" Cree asked with the raise of her eyebrow.

"My annoying ass mother," I replied as I ignored the call again.

"Wait, why you not picking up for her?" She questioned.

"Long story,"

"Well I have long time, so spill it," She said.

I started telling her about all the conversations that I've had with her over the last few months with her leaving her jaw dropped.

"OH, MY FUCKIN' GOD KERI, ARE YOU SERIOUS RIGHT NOW?" She asked astonished.

"As a fuckin' heart attack," I replied shaking my head.

"I can't believe the shit you just told me, as long as her bills were paid she didn't give a fuck about you and your safety, who the fuck does and says shit like that?"

"She does obviously," I replied disgusted silencing my phone again.

"Man, this shit just left a sour taste in my mouth," Cree said sipping her wine.

"Right,"

"Just answer it might be an emergency by the way she keeps calling," Cree suggested.

"Uggg fine, if she calls again," I replied rolling my eyes.

Phone vibrates….

"There you go," Cree laughed.

"Hello mother," I spoke as soon as I picked up.

"OH MY GOD KERI, THANK GOD YOU PICKED UP, COME TO YOUR HOUSE, SOMETHING HAPPENED TO MAX," She yelled frantically in the phone.

"Ma, calm down. What are you saying?"

"MAX IS DEAD KERI, COME HOME NOW,"

"Dead? What? How?" I questioned.

"I don't know I came to the house and fond him dead on the floor,"

"Why did you go there in the first place? You know what never mind. Did you call 911?" I asked.

"No, I called you first," She admitted.

"Why?"

"Because you're his fiancé Keri, why do you think? I thought you would want to be here," She cried.

"Well I'm sorry I can't help you, and I'm not his fiancé anymore. I'm going to hang up now so you can call who you need to call and get the proper help that you need for him, and please don't call me again," I stated hanging up the phone.

"Ummm what was all that about?" Cree asked looking concerned.

"Max is dead," I told her calmly.

"OH MY GOD KERI, why the fuck are you sitting here so calmly?" Cree yelled.

"Because Max dying has nothing to do with me, I've washed my hands of him and I refuse to go back down that road with him again dead or alive, she needs to be calling 911 and his parents to let them know not me. I can't be any help to them," I told her honestly.

"I hear you, are you okay?" She asked.

"Peachy," I replied with a smile sipping on my wine.

"You are one cold hearted bitch," Cree laughed.

"Not at all, I still care just not about him. He put me through a lot of shit over the years and he basically reaps what he sows. I'm not his wife so he isn't my concern," I simply stated.

"I hear that," She continued to laugh as she sipped on her wine.

We continued having girl talk and laughing like we been was doing before getting that phone call. In the back of my mind though I couldn't wait to see Cobain because I'm pretty sure that he had something to do with Max dying.

***

"Let Me ask you a question Cobain," I spoke sitting up in the bed and leaning on the headboard.

"Of course, you can get some more you already know you don't have to ask," He said licking his lips making my pussy throb.

"No, you jerk that's not want I want," I laughed hitting him on the arm.

"Well after the round we just had what else could be on your mind right now?" He asked as he sat up in the bed reaching over for his blunt.

"Seriously babe,"

"Did you have something to do with Max's death?" I asked looking over at him.

He took a pull of his blunt and didn't release it right away, he looked over at me and then finally released a cloud of smoke into the air.

"Do you really want to know?" He asked.

"Not really," I shrugged.

"Good, because I wasn't going to tell you anyway," He replied taking another pull of his blunt.

I just rolled my eyes and got out the bed and walked towards the bathroom, I don't even know why I bothered to ask him I knew his as wasn't going to tell me shit anyways.

"Damn doc just looking at you is making my dick hard all over again. You sure we can't get another round in before you leave?" He called out.

"Nope," I replied sticking my head out the bathroom door laughing.

I looked at my refection in the mirror and for the first time in a long time I felt happy and contempt with my life. I felt not one ounce of regret in my life and for that I was appreciative. I turned on the shower and got in quickly washing so I could hurry up and get out so I could get my day started.

After about fifteen minutes I was getting out the shower and wrapping the towel around my body and walking out the bathroom grabbing my clothes off the chair on the way.

"Aye doc let me ask you a question," Cobain requested.

"Okay, what's up?" I questioned as I was getting dressed.

"Where do you see yourself in five years?"

"Oh, that's easy eventually I want to own my own practice, and be my own boss," I told him truthfully.

"I like that, I see how your eyes light up when you just spoke about it. knowing you it will happen for you, your determined to make it in this world," He told me making me blush.

"You see that for me?"

"I see a lot for you in the future including being my wife and the mother of my son," He stated in a matter of fact tone.

"Oh, really now?" I asked shockingly.

"Hell yeah doc, I told you that your mine and I plan on building a future with you,"

"I hear you babe," I chuckled.

"You need to listen to what I'm telling you, mark my words Dr. Wade,"

"Dr. Wade huh?"

"It has a nice ring to it doesn't it doc?" He smirked.

"Yeah it does," I blushed putting on the rest of my clothes.

I leaned over and kissed him quickly but he had other plans as he pulled me on the bed and deepened the kiss.

"Mmmmmmm," I moaned into his mouth.

"Don't start nothing you can't finish doc," He spoke in between kisses.

"I'm not that's why I need to go now," I laughed as I gave him one last kiss.

"Damn doc, you got me wanting you to not even go anywhere right now,"

"I'll be back," I blew a kiss as I walked out the bedroom.

I went down the stairs and walked out the house, I was going to meet Khloe at the mall for a little girl talk and shopping on me of course. I jumped into my car and pulled out the driveway and went straight to the mall. I turned on the radio and let Drake blare through the speakers as I thought my past and my future. Since Cobain brought it up I thought it would be a good idea to get my plans in order. It would be a dream come true if I could have my practice sooner than the five years.

I pulled into the mall and found a parking spot right by the entrance which I was happy about because I definitely didn't feel like walking far. I got out and headed inside and went straight to Guess to me my sister. I walked in the store and saw her going through the racks and I couldn't do anything but smile, just a little while ago I thought I wouldn't never see her again.

"Hey Khloe," I said walking over to her.

"Heyyyyy," She replied hugging me with a smile.

"Found anything you like?" I asked as I looked at the items in her hands.

"Just a few things," She laughed.

"I bet,"

We walked around the store picking up things and trying them on, I always enjoyed shopping with Khloe she always made me feel young again. After we were done in Guess, we ended up in H&M, then Old Navy, Forever21, and a few other stores in the mall just wasting time and spending all my money. I didn't mind it though because I had enough of it since I hardly ever spent my own money, Max always made sure my account was full especially after his fuck ups.

We were sitting in the food court eating and laughing with all of our bags.

"I don't think I need to shop again for the next year," I joked.

"Speak for yourself," She laughed.

I drank some of my milkshake and put it back on the table and just looked at my sister. She was so pretty and looked so much healthier then she once did before and I couldn't be any more happier than I am at this moment.

"Listen I need to tell you something,"

"What's wrong? You okay?" She rattled off.

"Calm down I'm fine," I laughed.

"Good, so what's up then?"

"I don't know how you're going to take this but… Max is dead," I blurted out.

"Oh, that's it?" She asked.

"I mean yeah, how do you feel about that?" I questioned.

"Honestly I'm happy he's dead. I know that's not right but I'm not over what he did to us, and I probably never will be able to forgive him. So, it's better off that he's dead, he was dead in my eyes already anyway," She shrugged.

I was actually shocked at her response and wasn't expecting that at all but what could I really say about it though, he brought it all on himself with his latest stunts.

"Have you heard from mom?"

"Yeah, but I haven't been playing her to close lately. I'm just over everything right now and don't need the negativity in my life right now and that's all she is, and in order for me to completely heel I need to rid my life of all toxic people," She admitted.

I didn't say anything I just nodded my head and sipped my drink. I'm glad she was able to see for herself and I didn't have to tell her.

"If you choose to talk to her in the future, I support you but I don't want anything to do with her again. So just don't mention me to her she is dead to me," I told her straight up.

"Got it,"

"Thank you," I smiled.

"I love you Keri, even when I don't tell you, I do and I appreciate everything you've ever done or sacrificed for me to make sure I was good," She spoke sincerely.

"Aww Khloe, I love you too babe, you already know that though," I winked and smiled.

We sat there talking and laughing while we finished off the rest of our food, as soon as we were about to get up we heard a voice call our names.

"Ms. Keri… Khloe,"

We both turned and that's when we saw Kaylee and her mom coming our way.

"Great," I mumbled.

"Hi Ms. Keri," Kaylee sang out running into me.

"Hi baby girl, how are you?" I asked hugging her.

"Good," She smiled.

"That's good to hear,"

"Khloeeeeee," She shouted running into her with her eyes lit up.

They were so cute, Kaylee really looked up to Khloe it was so cute. Whenever we were altogether she made it her business to be up under her.

"Hi," Shyne spoke.

"Hello," I replied ready to walk to away.

"Can I talk to you for a minute please?"

"I don't have time, we were just about to leave," I told her not really in the mood for her shit today.

"Please, it will only be a minute," She pleaded.

"Fine,"

"First off, I want to say that I'm sorry about everything, I shouldn't have pulled that gun out on you and Cobain. It was very messy and I shouldn't have done that. Second, I want to apologize for what happened at his house that day, I was just being petty and as usual it backfired. I've loved Cobain for as long as I could remember so to see his attention elsewhere brought out a different side of me that I'm not proud of. I've done a lot of stuff over the years and after this last time we sat down and had a talk and we've come to middle ground," She explained.

"I'm glad to hear that and thank you for the apology," I responded.

"Cobain really loves you," She spit out.

"Excuse me?" I asked confused.

"He loves you, like really loves you. He loves you how I wish he loved me. When he sees your name pop up on his phone his eyes light up and I swear his heart skips a beat, it's kind of sickening knowing that it's not me that can make him feel that way. I'll probably always love him but I think I've had enough embarrassment to last me a life time. It's time for me to put my big girl panties on move on like I should have done years ago. He doesn't want me and I'm finally okay with that," She explained.

"Wow,"

"You won't have any issues from me anymore. You have my word," She stated.

"Well thank you for that, I can't say that I forgive you right now but I do respect you for owning up to your faults," I stated.

She smiled and nodded, I was still shocked at this whole situation right now.

"Thanx for listening,"

"No problem," I smiled.

"Come on Kaylee," She called out.

"Bye Ms. Keri, I'll text you later," She said skipping towards her mom as she waved.

"Bye Kaylee, okay," I responded laughing.

"That was awkward," Khloe mumbled.

"Tell me about it, let's go home," I said looping my arm through hers.

"Home, it sounds so good when you say that," She laughed.

"Doesn't it, it was a long time coming," I laughed with her as we headed out the mall.

Chapter 27- Cobain

3 months later...

"Keri let's go, we are going to miss our reservations," I yelled up the stairs for her to come on.

"I'm coming one more minute babe," She replied.

"You said that twenty minutes ago Keri, let's go now or I'm going to leave you. I'm hungry now girl,"

"Didn't you eat enough already? Her smart ass responded.

"I can eat that all night, but a nigga can't survive off your pussy alone no matter how good it is," I shouted.

"Okay, I'm coming," She laughed.

A few minutes later I finally heard heels clicking as she made her way down the steps and when I turned and saw how she looked a nigga was speechless.

"How do I look?" She asked once she reached the bottom of the steps and twirled so I could get a full view of her outfit.

"Damn doc, you are breathtaking," I stated pulling her in for a hug.

"Thank you, baby, was it worth the wait?"

"Most definitely," I replied kissing her.

"Told ya," She smirked.

"Tell me in the car before we are late," I told her as I slapped her on the ass.

"Okay, let's go,"

"Later I'm getting all up in that pussy, you showing out tonight, and I want you to keep the heels on," I told her.

"I hear you daddy," She seductively said sticking her tongue out at me.

"And the neighbors are about to hear you," I replied as we walked out the door.

I locked the door behind me and grabbed Keri's hand as we walked down the steps and to the car. I opened the car door for her and watched as she slid her sexy ass inside.

"Damn," I mumbled to myself.

I closed the door behind her and walked to the other side and got in the driver side. I put the car in drive and pulled off.

"Doc real talk you got my dick hard as fuck, I might have to take you in the bathroom of the restaurant for a quickie when we get there," I told her half-jokingly.

"You are so stupid," She laughed not knowing that if I could get away I was taking it.

I turned on the music and played some old school Plies for her and started rapping to her.

"*She got me speeding in the fast lane, pedal to the floor mayne trying to get back to her love, best believe she got that good thing, she my little hood thing, ask around they know us, they know that's my bust it... babyyyy,*"

"If I wasn't married to the streets it would be you, your lips what make you so cute, love when you poke your mouth out when you're mad too, save your name in my phone as lil boo, like your *sex but more in love with what you do, turn me on how you stare at me when we through, when you give it to me I don't wanna turn you lose, scared to moan around you all I say is "oh" my favorite panties are the ones that's see through, one with the pink trim on 'em and they light blue, speakin' for the goons thank god for makin' you BUST IT BABY is what I call you"* I rapped along to the song pointing in between us making her blush.

"That's how you really feel?" She asked cutting the music down.

"I guess you can say that,"

"Mmm" She replied.

"Mmm what?" I questioned.

"Nothing baby,"

"Yeah okay doc don't play with me," I squeezed her thigh.

"I'm not, I promise," She yelled as she tried to loosen the grip I had on her leg.

"Just making sure," I smirked letting go of her leg.

"You're such an asshole, that shit hurt," She whined as she rubbed her leg.

"I'm sorry, I'll kiss it for you later,"

"Oh, I know," She stated in a matter of fact tone.

We pulled up to the restaurant and I pulled straight into valet and put the car in park, I got out and walked around to Keri side and opened the door for her.

"Thank you,"

I grabbed her hand and we both walked inside the restaurant and up to the hostess.

"Hello and welcome do you have reservations?" She asked.

"Yes, under Wade please,"

"Ah yes, your party is already here and waiting, follow me," She acknowledged.

"Party? What is she talking about?" Keri asked looking at me.

I didn't respond I just grabbed her hand and followed the hostess to our table. I had us on the patio overlooking the water and the city lights. We walked through the crowed restaurant to our seats.

"OH MY GOD, WHAT ARE YOU ALL DOING HERE?" She screamed when she saw everyone here.

I had invited Ali, Cree, Kaylee, and Khloe, for this little surprise I was cooking up for her. She ran over and gave everyone a hug still in shock.

"What are they doing here?" She looked at me and asked.

"I figured we would just make this a family dinner," I shrugged.

"Aww thank you baby," She said kissing me.

"You know I'll do anything to make you smile," I stated.

I walked her over to her chair and pulled it out for her to sit, then pulled out the chair next to her.

"Ms. Keri, you look really pretty," Kaylee told her.

"Aww thank you princess, you look very pretty yourself," Keri replied to her.

It made me feel really good knowing that my girl and my daughter got along the way they did. That was very important to me, she would text Keri all day if I didn't tell her to chill.

"Why didn't you tell me you were going to be here?" I heard her ask Cree.

"Hell, I didn't know, he just told me we were going to dinner," She admitted.

"I couldn't tell you, you can't hold water when it comes to the doc so I just didn't tell you, y'all love surprises anyway so what's the big deal?" Ali smart ass said.

"Shut up please, I'm talking to my girl NOT you," She rolled her eyes at him.

"You been real snappy lately, you need some daddy dick Cree?" Ali asked quietly making her chocolate skin turn red.

"Do you," I threw out there laughing.

"Shut up Keri and mind your damn business,"

The waitress came and took our food and drink order then left us by ourselves. The night was beautiful and the view of the city added to the already amazing ambiance. I looked around the table and was happy at how everything turned out, I was surrounded by my family and couldn't be more grateful.

"Daddy can we do it now?" Kaylee asked trying to whisper.

"Really Kaylee," I laughed at this child of mine.

"What is she talking about? Is she okay?" Keri asked concerned looking between the both of us.

"She's fine," I replied shaking my head.

I was going to kick her ass when I got her home, I told her it was a secret clearly, I forgot who I was talking to. I already had this shit planned out and she was ready to ruin it with her impatient ass. The waitress came back over with our drinks and placed them down in front of everyone.

"I'd like to make a toast," I announced as I picked up my glass, I looked around and watched as everyone picked up their glass also.

"I just want to say I'm happy to have a small circle of family that I know I can count on at any given time. We not perfect but we real and I couldn't ask for anything more. I'm not really big on speeches so you know that means a lot coming from me," I joked.

"Cheers," They all said clinking the glasses and drinking their drinks.

"What the fu-"I heard Keri say.

She had spit something out her mouth from her drink into her hand and was looking at whatever it was.

"What's that Cree asked?"

She didn't speak she just looked up at me with tears in her eyes.

"What… what is this?" She asked barely above a whisper.

I took the ring from her hand and dried it off then I grabbed her hand and kissed it before saying what was on my mind.

"It's like this ma, I love you. I know we have yet to tell each other verbally but our actions show the love each day. Before I met you, I was just existing for Kaylee and not living my life to the fullest. You make me a better man and I want to see how much better I can be with you by my side," I started.

"Cobain," She whispered.

"In the words of my man Nipsey Hussle words gone fail me now… but my actions speak volumes. My job was to make you comfortable enough to be yourself with me… mission accomplished… I love who you are and respect how you hold shit down. Thanks for giving me the confidence to love you unconditionally, you know a nigga was raised to be skeptical. We just getting started though," I laughed.

She laughed through the tears along with me, as Kaylee handed her a tissue. She patted her eyes and took a deep breath.

"I just wanna know will you marry me doc?" I finally got out.

She nodded her head up and down as the tears continued to fall from her eyes.

"What's that doc I don't think Khloe heard you back there, you gon' ride with a nigga?"

"YESSSSSSSSSSS," She shouted.

I slid the ring in her finger and picked her up and kissed her passionately as I spun her around.

"SHE SAID YES DRINKS ON ME," I yelled through the restaurant causing everyone applaud and congratulate us.

She looked back at Khloe and I caught the look that they gave each other. So, I decided to let her in on a secret.

"I asked Khloe how she felt about me asking you to be my wife, and she's cool with it. We had a real adult like conversation, and she told her worry for you and I promised her that I would forever have both of y'all backs," I reassured her.

"Thank you,"

"No biggie ma, besides if she would have said no then this wouldn't be going on right now." I admitted shocking her.

I wiped the tears from her eyes and kissed her on the tip of her nose.

"Oh my God, I'm so happy for you," Cree shouted interrupting our moment pulling her towards the ladies.

"Thank you," I heard her say.

She hugged Cree then Khloe a little longer, I'm sure they were having a moment of their own. Then she looked down and picked up Kaylee kissing her on the cheek and hugging her, I was so happy I finally found the woman of my dreams. The waitress came back with our food and we all sat back down at the table and continued on with the celebration.

I grabbed Keri's hand and kissed it again, I couldn't keep my hands or eyes off her. She was just so beautiful to me and now she was about to be my wife. We were all having idle conversations across the table when Cree spoke up.

"I'm pregnant," She blurted out looking over at Ali.

"What?"

"I'm pregnant, I'm sorry Ali," She started to say.

"What are you apologizing for?"

"I'm just not sure how you would feel about me having a baby now," She admitted.

"When did you find out?" He asked looking at her.

"Today, I've been feeling sick so I took a test earlier when you left out,"

"For one stop being sad I'm not mad, I'm actually happy as fuck. I was starting to think my sperm wasn't working because you haven't gotten pregnant yet," He stated.

"What?" She asked confused.

"I was trying to get you pregnant, if you thought you was ever going to leave you had another thing coming, that baby was my insurance," He said seriously.

"Oh my God Ali, I can't believe you,"

"I can," I laughed.

"Well it looks like another round of congratulations are in order," Keri said picking up her glass of wine.

"Did you order a virgin drink Cree?" Ali asked grabbing her glass and sniffing it.

"Damn already he's on one," I laughed.

"Good luck Cree," Keri laughed.

"What you telling her good luck for? Soon as we get home I'm putting Kyle in you," I told her in a matter of fact tone.

"Who is Kyle?" She questioned

"Kaylee's little brother better known as my son, better get with the program,"

"Anyway, to Ali and Cree and their new blessing," Keri toasted ignoring me.

Again, we all toasted and sipped on our drinks and dug into our food. I sat back and looked at the table. I was surrounded with nothing but genuine love, a year ago if you would have told me I would be sitting here engaged and talking about another baby I would have probably shot you for talking shit.

"Who would have thought me engaged to be married and you engaged and expecting a baby on the way Ali?" I asked.

"Hell not me, I was supposed to be a player for lifeeeeee," He joked.

Cree looked at him and rolled her eyes making us all laugh.

"I'm just joking baby," He laughed kissing her and rubbing her stomach.

"Whatever,"

"Nah real shit though thank you for this, you changed my life more then you will ever know and I will spend eternity showing you how much I love you and am grateful for you giving me another chance at this thing called life," He said seriously.

"I love you too," She responded as she pulled him closer and kissed him.

"Awwwwww," Keri and Khloe said in unison which prompted Cree to give them the finger.

This night turned out better than I could have ever imagined, Kaylee came and sat on my lap and ate my food from my plate. I kissed her on the cheek as she dug into my plate. I grabbed Keri's hand never wanting to let it go. She turned and winked at me before continuing her conversation with the girls. I felt like the happiest man alive couldn't anything or anyone steal the joy that I felt in my heart right now, everything that I ever needed was right here at this table.

Epilogue

One year later...

Cree

Ali and I welcomed a bouncing beautiful baby boy into the world who we rightfully named Ali Jr. or Aj for short. He was definitely the man of the house and gave Ace and I a run for our money since the day he was born. He made his debut on the day Ali and I decided to get married. We woke up one morning and I decided that I didn't want the big fancy wedding or the hoopla and that I just wanted to marry the love of my life that day before our son came, I wanted to have his last name and he agreed so we got up and went down to the courthouse with Keri and Cobain and made it official. As soon as we said I do and kissed my water broke right there in the room. We all got out of there as fast as we could and heading straight to the hospital. I guess he felt because I married daddy it was finally time to make his appearance known.

Now and forever we would be celebrating our wedding and baby boy's birthday on the same day. This year has been nothing short of amazing Ali and I were madly in love with each other and I opened my own interior decorating company and hired a small crew to help me run it when I wasn't there. I had a little daycare in the back for days when I brought him to work with me or whenever my staff couldn't find a sitter they were allowed to bring their child to work with them. My life has completely turned around since meeting Ali before him I was looking for love in all the wrong places dealing with different kinds of men and when I finally took a step back and realized my worth that's when Ali was able to come in and steal my heart without me even realizing what he was doing. He was the man of my dreams and even though I wasn't originally checking for him I'm happy he never gave up on me because he changed my life for the better and I was forever grateful for him and my son. Everything wasn't perfect and I'm sure it wouldn't always be good but he's perfect for me and that's all that matters.

Ali

Married life for me has been great surprisingly Cree has been amazing, she takes care of Jr and me like we are her top priority. I couldn't have asked for a better person to wear my last name. She completes me in ways that I didn't even know existed or let alone even needed. Her and my son were the best things I never knew I needed. I took a step back from the illegal life after my son was born just so I could focus more on the home life. I didn't want to miss too much of his life with all the late nights and early mornings that come with being in the game. After about six months of playing the home front I decided to open a cigar bar. We served the best alcohol and Cuban cigars money could buy. We had flat screen Tv's all over and it was just a cool relaxing grown man environment. My new business venture was called "Ali's Way" and with the help of my beautiful wife with her skills the place was a sight for sore eyes. I was happy with this decision to open shop I had something else to do and it was a good investment and it kept the money coming in. overall life for us was good, I missed the fast life at times but all that shit was put on the back burner when it comes to my wife and son that shit wasn't worth me leaving my family. I had big plans for them so I needed to be out of jail and alive for that to happen so this was a smart business move and I had my sons name on it also as part owner so this was his when he got older. Little did Cree know I was knocking her little ass up real soon so I could have me a pretty little chocolate princess with a head full of hair, then my life would really be complete.

Keri

This past year has been simply amazing, Cobain and I have been taking this time to build, grow and make money moves together. I never really realized how much on life I was missing out staying with Max, since being with Cobain I've been living my best life and not regretting a minute of it. I opened up my own practice Keri's Korner with the help of Cobain of course, and my girl Cree came in and did the whole office for me and it looks simply amazing my girl definitely had skills at what she did. I hired Khloe as the receptionist when she wasn't in school so she could learn responsibility and continue getting her life in order. Since Max has been gone I've seen a big change in Khloe all around her behavior and social skills have come a long way. Cobain is so good with her it's really an amazing sight to see, he took her under his wing as if she was his. Cobain is one of the greatest men that I have ever encountered and I thank God every day and night for bringing him into my life when he did. I have started going to therapy once a week just to talk about my past to make sure it stays there and doesn't interfere with my future with Cobain, I know I have issues when it comes to relationships and I still have unresolved issues when it comes to my mom and shit so I'm just making sure nothing boils over into my future. I still haven't spoken to my mom since the last time she called my phone to tell me about Max being dead and I don't plan on it either. Khloe occasionally speaks to her but not as much as before, she was still hurt about the stuff I told her that she allowed Max to do to us. Overall, I'm happier and healthier than I have been in a very long time and I owe that all to Cobain, he truly is the love of my life. Kaylee has been a great addition to my little family, I was so used to it being just Khloe and I that having another little female around has been great, seeing how she has Cobain wrapped around her little finger is funny as ever. This house is full of females and it drives him crazy but I know he wouldn't change it for the world. Shyne tries to be an adult and co-parent but sometimes I still have to check her, she thinks I don't know that she still tries to throw herself at him when they do pick ups and drop offs with Kaylee. She got one more time then I'm going to have to reach out and touch her so she can learn I'm not finna play with her. Other than that, I have no complaints about life. I'm happy and so is my family and that is all I care about; next stop will be marriage and starting our own family which I can hardly wait for.

Cobain

Things on my end have been great I was still holding the illegal business side down since Ali took the backseat to it which was cool with me. I knew he had to do what he had to do. I was slowly making my way out of it so that I could sit back and enjoy life with my loved ones while I still can. I was putting another one of my trusted guys in charge so I could just sit back and continue to watch the money come in. My life was slowly coming together the way I always imagined got my lady on my side along with my baby girl and Khloe, all I was missing was my little man and I would be really set. I had decided to open up a skating rink and made Kaylee and Khloe co owners so the money would be all of theirs so when they got older they had their own businesses. KK's skating rink will be up and running by the beginning of summer, we were all excited about this especially Khloe I think she just wanted to see boys, I was going to have to have a talk with her about that. If any guy thought he was about to come to my house for a date Ali and I were going to do him how Will Smith and Martin Lawrence did that kid on Bad Boys 2. Have him scared out his mind if he even thought he was going to touch Khloe. Keri didn't know that I was working hard to get her pregnant, I tossed out her pills out a while ago so I was just waiting for confirmation that she was. I was trying to be patient and wait for my son but time was ticking and a nigga was getting old I wasn't trying to be the old dad on the football field. I think she was already pregnant but she didn't want to tell me. She's been snappy as fuck lately getting an attitude with everyone and eating all my damn Twinkies and that pussy has been extra juicy. She couldn't tell me she's not, ima just sit back and wait until she decides she's ready but I know if she takes too long I was going to buy every got damn test in the store and make her piss on them all in front of me until I found out the truth. A nigga was growing impatient now. Life in the Wade residence has definitely had its shares of ups and downs as any relationship would have and I was okay with that because we are far from perfect but we are perfect for each other. It was only up from here and I couldn't wait to see what the future holds for us. What I do know for sure is that Keri was about to be Mrs. Keri Wade and we were about to be living like the hood Obamas. I've waited all my life to find my soulmate and now that I have her I wasn't letting her go, I was ready to go to war for and about her. We've overcame a lot just to be where we are now, I've seen Keri go from this shy timid jumpy woman to a more confident and a little cocky in her skin. I fell more in love with her every day the more I see her grow into the person I know she is supposed to be. Thank you for taking this ride with us through all the ups and downs and trials and tribulations. There were times that we didn't know if either of us couples were going to even make it but we pulled through and now we are living life the way were supposed to with our queens by our sides and couldn't nothing stop us now.

The End!

Made in the USA
Lexington, KY
13 November 2019